Squire Terence and the Maiden's Knight

D0582370

KINGFISHER
An imprint of Kingfisher Publications Plc
New Penderel House, 283-288 High Holborn
London WC1V 7HZ
www.kingfisherpub.com

First published in the United Kingdom by Kingfisher 2005
2 4 6 8 10 9 7 5 3 1

Text copyright © Gerald Morris 1998
Published by special arrangement with
Houghton Mifflin Company.

The right of Gerald Morris to be identified as the author of
the Work as been asserted by him in accordance with the
Copyright, Designs and Patents Act of 1988.

Cover illustration copyright © Sally Taylor 2005

All rights reserved. No part of this publication may be
reproduced, stored in a retrieval system or transmitted by
any means electronic, mechanical, photocopying or otherwise,
without the prior permission of the publisher.

A CIP catalogue record for this book
is available from the British Library.

ISBN-13: 9 780753 41032 5
ISBN-10: 0 7534 1032 X
Printed in India
1TR/1204/THOM/(SCHOY)/90NS/C

SQUIRE TERENCE AND THE MAIDEN'S KNIGHT

GERALD MORRIS

KINGFISHER

937,047/JF

CONTENTS

For Rebecca,
for more than I can say –
G.M.

1

TERENCE

Terence crept nervously through the forest, glancing often over his shoulder. He was a slim, agile boy, perhaps fourteen years old – though he did not know his age exactly – and he moved easily among the brambles. He had been prowling the woods since he could walk, gathering food for the hermit's meals. Today, though, the forest that had always been his home was strangely unfriendly.

He had gone out to check his snares, but from the moment he stepped into the woods, odd things had been happening. First, he stumbled over an ancient tree stump, which squatted in the centre of a path that had been clear just the day before. When he picked himself up and turned to examine the stump, it was gone. The wind through the trees sounded suspiciously like someone chuckling.

A few steps farther down the path, Terence saw a face. It was completely green and was framed by wild hair that seemed to be made of leaves and grass, but it was certainly a face: a small, triangular, impishly laughing face that disappeared a moment later. For a moment Terence stared; then he hurried away in a new direction. That had begun a frightening afternoon. A familiar oak had a new branch that, when touched, fell to the ground and slithered away like a snake. A squirrel sat on a rock beside the path and sang like a nightingale. A tortoise scurried by him, as quickly as a hare. And everywhere was that impish chuckle and that face.

Terence's fear grew with each passing minute. Once, looking over his shoulder, he walked right into a tree. Behind him a merry little voice chuckled and said, "Ho ho, little one. That one wasn't even me."

Terence started like a deer and ran, but the grinning face followed. At last he stumbled into a little clearing in the heart of the forest, and the voice said, "Right then, here you are. I've done with you for now." At once Terence felt the eerie presence withdraw. The forest was calm and pleasant and comfortably dull. He took a deep breath and gazed ahead.

Beneath a great oak in the centre of the clearing lay the largest man Terence had ever seen. Behind him, three huge horses cropped grass, and beside the man were a few scattered rabbit bones next to a smouldering fire. A broken snare, one of Terence's, lay nearby. Terence hesitated at the edge of the meadow.

"This your snare, boy?" the stranger asked without opening his eyes.

Terence jumped, but he answered, "Yes, sir."

"You'd do better hunting with a bow, but I can't complain. A meal is a meal." The man still had not moved.

"Yes, sir." Terence could think of nothing else to say.

"Come here, boy." As he spoke, the man sat up, and Terence saw his face. He was surprisingly young, perhaps only five or six years older than Terence himself. His red beard was still thin. He waved Terence over and picked up a bent staff with a string tied to both ends, and several shorter sticks. He handed them to Terence. "I owe you something for the rabbit. Would these do?"

Terence held them awkwardly, and the man's gaze sharpened. "Haven't you ever seen a longbow before?"

"No, sir."

The man stared, then took back the bent stick. In one swift motion he fitted one of the short sticks on the string, pulled it back, and released it. The stick flew across the clearing and stuck, quivering, in a dead log. Terence stared, and the man watched him sharply. "You really haven't seen one before, have you?"

Terence shook his head dumbly.

"Where are you from, boy?"

"I live with the hermit," he said.

"A hermit? A religious man?"

Terence nodded.

"Good Gog, son, why?"

"My parents left me on his step when I was a baby. He's raised me." The man looked at Terence consideringly, and Terence added, "I hunt for him and do all his cooking."

"If you hunt, then you need to learn how to use a bow. Let me show you. You hold it like this." For the next three hours, Terence learned how to hold the bow, to string the arrows, to hold and release the string, to aim, and how to care for the bow and the string. The stranger was a stern but patient teacher, and if he was quick to rebuke Terence's mistakes, he would also grunt a gruff approval when Terence did something right. At the end of the afternoon, Terence felt sure that he would never be any good with a bow, but to his surprise the man said, "You're a natural, son. I've never seen anyone do this well so quickly. Soon you'll be hitting rabbits on the run."

The big man began to gather his gear, preparing to go. "Please, sir," Terence stammered. "Thank you."

The man smiled. "You're welcome, lad. And besides, I don't like snares."

"It's late, sir," Terence continued. "Won't you come and stay the night at the hermitage? I'll cook your dinner."

"Eat with a religious man?" The man grinned ruefully and muttered, "What would Mother say?" but after a moment he nodded. "All right, lad. Lead the way." He whistled softly, and the horses trotted over to him. The largest one, a mountainous black horse with a wicked eye, the big man saddled. Then he began loading the other two.

Terence saw a gleaming coat of mail hung with solid metal plates. "Cor, sir! Are you a knight?"

The man grinned. "Not yet, but I plan to be if the king sees fit."

"Which king?" Terence asked. In those days, any great lord who controlled enough land was likely to call himself king.

"King Arthur, lad. The true king."

Terence gaped at him. "Is that where you're going, sir? To King Arthur?"

"No. I'm going to a scabby hermitage to let a scrubby brat cook my dinner. Lead the way, boy."

Getting Terence onto one of the packhorses took time, since he had as little experience with horses as he had with a longbow, but eventually they were under way. Terence was relieved to discover that his mount needed no guidance from him but instead had been taught simply to follow the lead horse. The big man led, with Terence calling out directions from behind.

As they drew near the hermitage, Terence said, "The hermit's name is really Trevisant, sir, but most people—"

He broke off. Next to a slender beech tree, not two yards to Terence's left, stood a small, green, slightly built figure who smiled pleasantly at Terence over a pointed beard. The figure doffed his cap politely, then disappeared, leaving only a wisp of green smoke rising through the branches. Terence choked.

"What is it, lad?" The big man was miraculously holding a sword.

Terence swallowed and said, "Nothing, sir. Sorry, sir."

The man's eyes followed Terence's toward the

beech, but all he said was, "All right."

When they rode into the clearing, the hermit was waiting for them. He extended his arms to the stranger. "Welcome, Sir Gawain – The Maiden's Knight."

The man stared. "Eh?"

"Oh no, you're quite right. I'm ahead of myself, aren't I?" the hermit said apologetically. "That comes later."

Terence wished he had thought to warn the big man. Terence hardly noticed the hermit's peculiarities anymore, but he could well imagine that they might be disconcerting to a stranger. Trevisant, the Hermit of the Gentle Wood, had been given a special gift many years ago. Where most people remembered the past and guessed at the future, Trevisant saw the future clearly but could remember only a few hazy details of the past. Of course, now that he was getting older – some said he was over a hundred years old, though of course Trevisant couldn't tell them – his memory was not what it used to be, and he was likely to forget even the future. Once, helping the hermit look for something he had misplaced for the third time in a day, Terence had said that this great gift of God was a terrible inconvenience sometimes. The hermit had laughed and said, "So are they all,

7

Terence. So are they all."

"Come in, come in, Sir Gawain," the hermit continued jovially. "Terence, I've packed your clothes already, so you won't have to bother with it. You can't imagine my surprise when I realized that this was the day you would leave. I must have known it, but it slipped my mind."

"Leave?" Terence stared.

"Sir Gawain, you can put your horses out back near the lightning-struck tree."

The stranger looked at him oddly, but said only, "Thank you, sir."

"There's no lightning-struck tree back there," Terence said.

"Hasn't that happened yet? Well then, where did we used to put horses, I wonder." The hermit frowned.

"There's a shed there," Terence said.

"What, is the shed still standing?" the hermit cried. "Then by all means use the shed. Terence, you'll need to start dinner."

Terence went inside. He wanted to ask the hermit what he meant about his leaving, but the old man had disappeared. Terence was mixing spices and adding a few vegetables to a hearty stew when the big man walked in.

"Hello, lad," he said. "That already smells

wonderful. How do you do it?"

Terence grinned and said, "I've had to learn. The hermit can't cook for himself, you know."

Before the man could answer, the hermit himself walked into the room, carrying a deerskin bag. "Don't be foolish, Terence. How do you suppose I managed before you came along, hey?"

Terence grinned. "I've often wondered, sir. How did you?"

"Well, you can't expect me to remember, can you?" In a softer voice, he added, "Don't worry about me, my son. I'll be taken care of when you're gone. Trust me. I know it."

"But sir," Terence said, "I'm not going anywhere."

"What? Don't you know yet?"

"No, sir."

"Oh, you're off to be Sir Gawain's squire."

Terence frowned at the big man. "Are you Sir Gawain, sir?"

"No, lad. Only Gawain. I haven't been knighted, remember."

"What? You haven't even been knighted yet?" the hermit exclaimed. "I'm all in a puzzle today, aren't I? Well, don't worry about it. When Arthur hears about Sir Hautubris, he'll knight you quick enough."

9

"Sir Who?" Gawain asked.

"Hautubris. No, no. No questions. Just wait."

"Milord," Terence began – somehow just "sir" was no longer enough – "you should know that the hermit sees time backwards. He sees the future the way we see the past and the past the way we see the future."

Gawain looked at the hermit thoughtfully and said, "It sounds like a terrible curse, sir."

"Oh, it has its moments," the hermit replied with a slight smile.

In a few minutes, Terence had placed three steaming bowls of stew on the bare wood table. The hermit blessed it, and all three ate ravenously. When the pot was empty, Gawain leaned his stool back against a wall and said, "Father, I have to argue with you about the future."

"Don't call me Father," the hermit said agreeably. "I'm not a priest."

"All right. Nevertheless—"

"And don't argue with me about the future, either. You can't win. You're about to say that you already have a squire, aren't you?"

"That's right. My brother—"

"Don't tell me about Gaheris. He's a clodpole, Sir Gawain. And you know it."

"Sir—" Gawain began resolutely.

"Can you deny that Gaheris is a clodpole?"

Reluctantly, Gawain smiled. "No, sir, but he's my brother."

"Good heavens," the hermit said shaking his head in amazement, "When I think of the Banlieu affair I don't know where that boy's wits have gone begging."

"The *what* affair?" Gawain leaned forward, his eyes bright.

"Oh, shouldn't I have said anything? Well, I can't help telling this one little story. Gaheris tells this knight, Sir Banlieu, that he'll fight any man alive but he'll never raise sword against the skirts of womanhood – or something like that. You know the way he talks."

"Ay, it sounds like him," Gawain said, his eyes gleaming.

"So, Sir Banlieu comes to fight wearing a skirt he's borrowed from some lady."

"I'd like to know how he got it," Gawain interjected.

"I can tell that, too, but I can see it won't do to tell you about it. Anyway, Gaheris won't fight. Banlieu pops him off his horse as easily as you please and ducks him in the horse pond."

"Well of all the cheek," Gawain said admiringly.

The hermit continued, "Anyway, putting aside

Gaheris's idiocy, you can't think that he would ever be able to cook a meal like this, can you?"

Gawain looked at Terence sharply, his eyes widening. "No, he wouldn't, for a fact."

"Then that's the end of it," the hermit said. "Good heavens, Sir Gawain, when I think of all the troubles you and Terence share, I can't believe you would even hesitate. Think of the shaughuses! Ah, but you can't, can you?"

"Poison eels?" Gawain asked. "What about them?"

"No no, I'm no penny-pinching soothsayer. You'll find it all out in good time." Gawain frowned abstractedly at Terence for a moment, and the hermit added in a gentler voice, "It's not just for your convenience, son. Terence also has work to do. He needs you as much as you need him."

Gawain's frown cleared, and he nodded. "How about it, lad? Would you like to be my squire?"

Terence looked hesitantly at the hermit.

"I told you, son. I'll be fine." Trevisant smiled at him. "But bless you for thinking of me."

Terence looked back at Gawain and said, "Yes, milord. I think I would."

"I'll have to teach you everything, won't I?" Gawain said. "You can't even ride."

"No, milord. But I can learn."

"Ay, I've seen that you can," Gawain said. "We'll leave in the morning."

A horse's hooves thudded out front, and a loud, harsh voice called, "You in the house!"

Terence started to get up, but Trevisant laid a hand on his arm and shook his head. "You go," he said to Gawain.

Gawain nodded and opened the front door. The light was growing dim, but through the door Terence saw a mounted knight in full armour.

"Can I help you?" Gawain asked politely.

"I need food. I've been smelling your meal for twenty minutes now, and I want some."

"Terribly sorry," Gawain said, "but we've just finished it. Terence," he called back, "do we have anything else we can give this hungry knight?"

"I don't want something else, my good man," the knight said. "Because I don't believe you. I can still smell food in there."

Swiftly, Gawain reached over the table to the stewpot. He held it upside down before the knight. "As you see, sir, the pot is empty."

"Are you being insolent, churl?" the knight demanded. "You'll taste my whip if you are."

Gawain shrugged, then took two quick steps forward. He heaved up on the horse's stirrup, and the knight clattered into a heap on the other side of the horse. Cursing, the knight clanked awkwardly to his feet.

"Now *that*," Gawain said, "was being insolent."

"You'll pay for that, villain," the knight snarled. "No forest churl lays hands on Sir Hautubris without blood."

"Sir Who?" Gawain asked sharply. He glanced at the hermit, who stood in the doorway.

"Yes, yes. This is the one. Watch your head," the hermit said.

Sir Hautubris flashed his sword from his scabbard and chopped down mightily at Gawain's head. Gawain stepped quickly to one side, and the sword buried itself in the dirt next to him. Gawain rapped Sir Hautubris's helm with the stewpot. The visor flopped up and down, and a loud clang rang out.

"Prepare to die, varlet!" Sir Hautubris cried, taking another full swing. Gawain moved slightly and again the sword buried itself in the ground. Gawain clanged the stewpot against the other side of the knight's head. His helm pivoted to the left, so that the right eyehole was over Sir Hautubris's nose.

"Curse it, where are you?" Sir Hautubris shouted. He swung his sword around him in a full roundhouse swing.

"Watch it, you fool!" Gawain called sharply. "You'll hit your horse." Gawain slipped inside the circular swing and plucked Sir Hautubris's sword from his hand. "You're not to be trusted with this thing," he said.

For a moment Sir Hautubris stood shakily in the centre of the yard, readjusting his helm so he could see. Gawain turned toward the hut, and Sir Hautubris tottered back to his horse. Terence sighed with relief, then gasped again, because Sir Hautubris had drawn another sword from the saddle and was charging Gawain's back. Terence tried to call a warning, but Gawain had already moved. Two swords flashed, and Sir Hautubris lay in the dust, his own sword in his breast.

"If I have to kill everyone who smells your cooking, lad, we're in for a long road," Gawain said.

Terence wept when he left the hermit. Gawain waited, patient and unembarrassed, while Terence embraced the old man and kissed him tearfully. Trevisant whispered in Terence's ear, "This is the nice thing about seeing time my way: no regrets," and pushed him gently away. "Now," he said to Gawain, "I haven't granted you a boon yet, have I?"

Startled, Gawain shook his head.

"Come here, then." Gawain stepped forward. "Kneel, boy. You're in the presence of more than you know. More than I know, actually." Stiffly, Gawain knelt in front of the Hermit of the Gentle Wood. "Sir Gawain, so long as you fight, your strength will grow with the sun. It is a gift. You may stand." Gawain rose. "Do you understand your gift?"

"No."

"As the sun rises, your strength will rise. At dawn, you will gain a new strength, which will reach its peak at noon."

"And, if I may ask, will my strength lower as the sun lowers?"

Trevisant chuckled. "No gift is exactly what we want, my son. Try to fight in the morning. And you, Terence." Trevisant held his hand up, palm out. "Serve your new master well. You will find your greatest glory in service." The three of them stood in the fresh morning breeze for a moment. Then Trevisant said, "Right then, off you go."

And as they passed through Terence's familiar forest on their way to King Arthur's court, Terence heard a soft, merry voice in his ear, whispering, "Godspeed, Terence."

2

KING ARTHUR'S COURT

The journey to King Arthur's new court at Camelot could have been made in less than a week, but Gawain and Terence took almost two. They travelled in the morning, and in the afternoons, Gawain trained his ignorant new squire. He taught him how to take care of armour and horses and how to fasten armour on a knight. It was Terence's job to look after Gawain's packhorses and his own horse, the one that had belonged to Sir Hautubris. Gawain himself always cared for his huge black stallion, Guingalet. When Terence offered to help, Gawain only laughed and said, "Nay, lad. Guingalet's an aughisky. He'd likely bite your arm off."

"What's an aughisky?"

"It's a water horse from Orkney. They live as

17

much in the sea as on land. They're the very devil to catch, but once mastered, there's no finer mount in the world. And I do think Guingalet's fond of me, now." He patted the horse's sleek neck, and Guingalet snapped at his hand.

Every day, Terence practised with his longbow. At first Gawain watched these sessions, but after the first few days he let Terence practise on his own. The first time that Terence brought home game that he had killed with the bow was a proud day. It was a large buck rabbit, and the arrow had pierced its body directly behind the front legs. Gawain examined it critically. "Just the right spot, Terence."

"Thank you, milord." Terence beamed proudly.

"How far away were you?"

Terence felt sheepish, but he told the truth. "Only about two yards, milord."

Gawain looked at him curiously. "Don't be ashamed of that, lad. Any number of men can shoot an arrow accurately, but not one in fifty can get that close to a full-grown rabbit."

"I could have gotten closer, but the bow snagged in the brush."

"Could you, now?" Gawain said. He looked at him pensively, then asked, "You don't have any notion who your parents were, eh?"

937,047/JF

"No, milord."

"Hmm." Gawain thought for a moment. "Well, that's neither here nor there. You've got the look."

"The look of what, milord?"

"You've faery blood in you. I'd swear to it. There's something in the eyes. And to see you sliding through the brush is like watching a ghost."

The hermit had never talked much about faeries, but Terence had heard of them from travellers who had stopped at the hermitage. Most of what he had heard had been about faeries doing mischief and luring people to their death. Gawain said, "It doesn't please you, boy?"

Terence swallowed. "No, milord."

"Why not?"

"Faeries are wicked, aren't they?"

"Some of them are. Some aren't at all. It's more than you can say of men." Terence still frowned, and Gawain added, "There's no shame in a touch of faery blood, Terence. I've some myself."

"You, milord?"

"On my mother's side. For that matter, so does the king."

"King Arthur?"

"Ay. Just like the rest of our family. My mother and my Aunt Morgan show it the most, but even that blundering gapeseed Gaheris has a bit."

WESTMEATH COUNTY LIBRARY

19

Terence blinked. "Milord, is the king a part of your family?"

"Ay, Terence, the king's my uncle."

Terence looked at him with awe. "Then you're almost a prince!"

Gawain laughed and said, "Better than almost, really. My father was King Lot of the Orkney Islands." Terence's eyes widened, and Gawain said hurriedly, "But don't go calling me Prince Gawain or some rot like that. Now that we have a King of All England, there is no more kingdom of Orkney. And a knightship at Arthur's court is a greater honour than any princedom. Knighthood has to be earned." Gawain shook his head briskly. "Are you going to cook that rabbit or watch it age?"

The next afternoon they met another traveller. They were about to stop when they heard a sharp chopping noise. Gawain narrowed his eyes and continued forward silently. A moment later, in a tiny clearing in the forest, Terence saw a tall, strong-looking young man wearing rough leather clothes and holding a heavy sword in his left hand. He stood completely still in front of an old tree, then suddenly sprang lightly to the right. His sword flashed out and buried itself in the trunk of the tree. Immediately the young man wrenched it free and took his position again.

"Milord?" Terence whispered. Gawain leaned close but did not answer. "What's he doing?"

Gawain lifted his eyebrows slightly. "Fighting a tree, of course."

"Oh." The young man sprang again, and again the sword flashed, sinking into the tree at exactly the same spot.

Gawain whistled. "Come on, Terence. Shall we meet this abuser of trees?" He tapped Guingalet lightly with one heel and pushed through the brush into the clearing. Behind a tree, Terence saw an ancient, broken-down cart horse and two leather packs on the ground. The young man turned, still holding his sword.

"Hello," Gawain said pleasantly.

"Who are you?" the young man answered abruptly.

Gawain paused briefly before answering. "No enemies of yours, I believe," he murmured.

The young man flushed. "I beg pardon for my rudeness."

"Given," Gawain said. He carelessly dismounted and said, "You have found yourself a fine camp here. Do you permit us to share it with you?"

The young man looked at Gawain suspiciously, but only said, "If you wish."

"Terence, see to the horses," Gawain called, sitting at the base of a tree. He turned back to the young man. "My name is Gawain."

"I am Tor," the young man replied stiffly. He sat near Gawain, still holding his sword in his left hand. Terence led the horses to one side, unobtrusively drawing his bow and an arrow. Gawain had left his sword in the scabbard on Guingalet's saddle.

"Where are you bound?" Gawain asked in that pleasant, conversational tone.

"Camelot!" Tor said defiantly, as if expecting Gawain to take offense.

"Really? Now that's where we're going, too. Have you business with the king?"

"I hope so," the young man said.

"Why, that's my case exactly," Gawain said, smiling. "I hope to be made a knight of the Round Table."

Tor relaxed slightly. "You're not a knight already?"

"Nay," Gawain said.

"Oh. I thought . . . when I saw your armour. . . ."

"Any clodpole can own armour," Gawain commented. Tor stiffened again, and half raised his sword. Terence swiftly strung his bow and notched an arrow, but Gawain continued calmly,

"And any number of good fighters have to do without it."

Tor relaxed again and laid his sword beside him. Gawain reached into his blouse, pulled out a handful of hazelnuts, and began cracking them. "Have one?"

Tor nodded, and Gawain flipped a nut at him. Tor caught it deftly in his right hand, cracked it, and began eating.

"Do you hope to be made a knight as well?" Gawain asked.

Again Tor stiffened. "Why do you ask that?"

"I saw you practising. If you'll take a word of advice, don't practise on trees. Nothing blunts iron like wood."

Tor blushed but answered steadily, "I had nothing else . . . or no one else . . . to practise on."

"Yes, that would be difficult. Now me, I had my brothers. Not that they were much more competition than a tree, but at least they didn't blunt my sword. You see," Gawain added, "I was careful not to hit their heads."

Tor's face lightened and a tiny dimple appeared on his cheek. "That was kind of you," he said.

"No no, not at all. I did it to save my sword."

"Would you like to practise on me?" Tor asked,

half defiantly, half shyly. "I would be glad of the chance."

"Then you'd be a fool," Gawain answered. "Never offer to fight an unknown, Tor. Now you don't know the first thing about me."

"You don't know anything about me, either," Tor pointed out.

"On the contrary. You're right-handed, but you'd probably start with your left hand, then shift to your right. You rely on speed, which is good, but your weakness is probably your return swing. If I were fighting you, I would play to your weak side to force you to keep shifting hands, and I would try to interfere with your exchanges. It shouldn't be too hard to knock your sword down soon. Have another hazelnut."

Tor let out his breath in a long, slow sigh. "You saw all that, and you're not even a knight yet!" he said. Gawain said nothing. In a moment, Tor said bitterly, "I'm reaching for the moon."

"Nothing wrong with that," Gawain said. "Here, Terence, you bloodthirsty cub, put down your bow and see about some food for us."

Meekly, Terence stepped out from behind the horses, still holding his bow with his arrow notched. Gawain grinned. "You'll do, lad. Tor, this is my squire, Terence."

Tor looked at Terence's bow with surprise. "What's that for?"

Terence swallowed. "I thought you might not be friendly, sir."

Tor shook his head. "I could have been dead twice over today, and I never even knew I was in danger."

The next day, by mutual unspoken consent, the three rode off together. By early afternoon they could tell that they were nearing Camelot. They began to pass drovers and shepherds and carriers in slow ox-carts. Then they began to see knights, all fully armed and armoured. Twice they pulled off the road to let galloping regiments pass, and once they rode by a surly band of armed peasants. Gawain was frowning darkly.

"Gawain?" Tor asked quietly. "Have you heard anything about a war?"

"Looks like it, doesn't it?" Gawain said. "Yeomen with weapons, knights in regiments, wagons filled with provisions."

The three travellers rounded a bend, and there was Camelot, perched high on a hill overlooking the plain to the south and east. It seemed to Terence to be carved right out of the rock, a dark, solid castle festooned with gay banners. A steady stream of horsemen and cattle and wagons wound up the hill to the front gates. On the plain below Camelot hill, parties of horsemen formed lines and galloped in circles and blew trumpets and shouted at each other. Finally they came to the gate, where a thick, dark-bearded man was meeting the carts of provisions, allowing some to pass and sending some away. As they watched, one of the carters began to argue shrilly about being sent away, and a moment later the carter rose through the air and landed with a wet thump in his cart full of unpleasant-smelling cabbages.

"That was quick," Gawain murmured to Tor. "This dark fellow is no mere servant or guard."

As Gawain spoke, the dark-bearded man beckoned for them to approach. "What have we here?" he asked softly.

"Two who would be knights of the Round Table," Gawain answered. The dark-bearded man looked at Tor, then Terence. He cocked one eyebrow quizzically. "And one who would be the squire of a knight of the Round Table," Gawain added.

The man scratched his beard and regarded them sourly. "Your names?"

"Tor and Gawain."

The man looked at him sharply. "Gawain?" Gawain bowed slightly. "Hmm. You with us or against us?"

"With you."

The man grunted. "Right then. Stable your horses. Tell the grooms that Sir Kai sent you. Arthur's holding council tonight; you can talk to him then." With a wave of his hand, Sir Kai motioned them on and turned his attention to a cart filled with scrawny chickens.

Terence had never seen so many people or so many bright colours at one time in his life. He saw tall ladies in elegant flowing gowns; chunky, bearded dwarfs in leather waistcoats; knights with painted armour, plumed helms, and intricately designed shields. (Gawain grunted, "Show-warriors.") They watched knights sparring with swords, and saw cooks roasting whole oxen over huge fires. At last they found the stables, saw to their horses, and stretched out on a haystack.

Gawain told Tor and Terence all that he knew about Arthur: how he was the true son of the old king, Uther Pendragon, but had been raised as an orphan by Sir Ector, who was Sir Kai's father, and how he had become king by drawing the Sword Excalibur from the stone. He told them of Arthur's wars to establish his right to the throne, and how finally almost every part of Britain had vowed fealty to him.

"Oh," Terence said. "That's what you meant when you said that there was no more kingdom of Orkney. Your father vowed fealty to Arthur."

Gawain looked grim. "Nay, Terence. That he did not. But my father is dead now."

Tor looked at Gawain shrewdly. "He died in battle?" he asked. Gawain nodded. "So that's why the man at the gate – Sir Kai – asked you if you were with the king or against him. Your father fought against Arthur, didn't he?"

"And my mother," Gawain said with a nod.

"And, forgive me if I ask too many questions, but where is your mother now? Has she vowed fealty to Arthur?"

Gawain hesitated, then said, "I do not know where my mother is. I have chosen to follow Arthur instead. Though I've never met him myself, I know him for a true king. Remember, he defeated my father. If you want to know a king, see how he treats his defeated foes. All are gracious to their equals; one in a thousand is gracious to an enemy he has conquered."

When Terence finally saw King Arthur for himself, he understood Gawain's admiration. At dusk, in an open courtyard, King Arthur feasted with his court. Behind him, minstrels sang a long ballad about an ancient hero named Cucholinn, and all around him knights and ladies-in-waiting talked and dallied elegantly. Gawain and Tor sat on a long bench opposite the throne, and Terence, following Gawain's whispered instructions, stood behind Gawain. At first, Terence thought that Arthur looked too young to be the King of All England, but there was dignity in his bearing and wisdom in his eyes. Terence had never seen a king before, but he knew that this was how one should look.

When the meal was finished, King Arthur held his hand up, and like magic, the room became silent.

"And now we shall hold court," he said. "Kai?"

The dark-bearded man from the gate stood. "Here."

"How are we provisioned?"

"Adequately. Unless the Five Kings have resources that we don't know about, we can outlast them in the field by about a week. Two weeks, with a bit of foraging."

"One week will do," Arthur said gently. "We wish to rule our people, not ruin them." Kai bowed slightly. "Thank you, Kai. I believe I have given you an arduous job, but you have done it well." Kai's hard, craggy face flushed darkly, and he bowed again, more deeply. "Come stand by me, Kai," Arthur continued. "I shall need your counsel." Kai stepped up to Arthur's throne, a fierce pride in his face.

"Tomorrow," the king said, speaking to the whole room, "we shall go to war against the Five Rebel Kings. Is there anyone here who would not go with us?" A deathly hush fell on the room. It seemed to Terence as if everyone had turned to stone. The king waited for a full minute, then said, "Very well," and everyone breathed again. Arthur grinned, looking for a moment like a mischievous boy, and turned to a greying knight at his left. "Sir Ector?"

"Yes, your highness?"

"You and your knights will stay behind tomorrow to guard Camelot. Should we come to grief, you will act as regent for the kingdom. Do you understand?"

"Yes, your highness. But—" The knight swallowed and stopped.

"But what, Father?" the king asked.

The familiar title seemed to give Sir Ector courage. He said, "Is there no one else who could stay here?"

"There are many who could, but none whom I could trust so fully," Arthur replied.

Sir Ector flushed and bowed, as Kai had done, and said, "As you wish, my king."

Terence understood more than ever Gawain's admiration for King Arthur. Sir Ector and Sir Kai, Arthur's own adopted father and older brother, would clearly consider it an honour to die for their young sovereign.

"We leave at dawn, then," Arthur said. "Is there anything else for us to deliberate this evening?"

Gawain leaned forward, and Tor fidgeted, but neither spoke. Sir Kai cleared his throat and said, "There is one other matter that I know of, Arthur."

"Yes, Kai?"

"Two men joined us this afternoon wishing to be made knights of the Round Table."

"Are these men here?" the king asked.

Sir Kai nodded at Gawain and Tor, and they stood. Arthur looked at them thoughtfully, then nodded at Tor. "Come ahead, friend."

Tor stepped forward and knelt at the king's feet. Arthur said, "Rise, friend. Tell me your name."

"I am Tor, your highness," he said, standing.

"Where are you from?"

"From Hartsbeck Heath, your highness."

"And who are your parents?"

Tor's chin lifted stubbornly, and he said in a

31

ringing voice, "My father is Aries the Cowherd, and my mother is named Kate." A hubbub of surprised conversation rose, and Arthur quelled it with his hand.

"Why do you want to be a knight, Tor?"

"It is all I am good for, your highness. I have no love for cattle, no interest in farming. My dreams have always been with the knights." A hush spread over the room, and Tor added quietly, "I have my father's leave to seek my fortune here."

"It is good you said so," Arthur said approvingly. "I would not have any son desert his father."

"To be honest, your highness, he said that I might as well leave, since I was useless to him."

Arthur laughed an easy, pleasant laugh. "Well said, Tor! Have you ever done a deed deserving of knighthood?"

"No, your highness."

"Then even if I want to, I cannot knight you. One must earn the right of knighthood at my table." Tor bowed and started to back away, but an old man in a black shawl, standing slightly behind Arthur, cleared his throat and said, "Your highness?"

Arthur turned and looked at the old man. "Yes, Merlin?"

So this was Merlin! Even in the hermitage,

Terence had heard of the great enchanter. The aged magician said, "I don't mean to interfere, but you don't want to lose such a knight as this youth will become."

Arthur looked thoughtfully at Tor while the court buzzed. One voice sounded louder than the others, saying, "But the son of a cowherd?"

Merlin spoke clearly. "It is from that honest cowherd that Tor learned his courage, strength, and goodness. You see that the boy himself declares the name of Aries proudly. It is well and justly done."

Arthur spoke clearly, "Only a fool disregards Merlin. What I will do, Tor, is allow you to ride with me to the wars tomorrow. You shall be given your chance to earn what you desire."

Tor bowed again. Sir Kai leaned over and whispered in Arthur's ear. He nodded and spoke once more, "And Tor, I hope that you will let me provide you with a mount."

Tor flushed with pleasure but said, "I have a horse, your highness."

The king smiled. "But it has just completed a long journey. It deserves its rest."

"Then I can only say thank you, your highness," Tor said and took his seat again. Arthur looked at Gawain, and Gawain stepped forward.

"And what is your name, friend?"

"Gawain."

The king's head jerked up, and he stared at Gawain eagerly. "Gawain? Of Orkney?"

"Yes, sire."

"Nephew!" Arthur cried. He leaped forward and embraced Gawain, kissing him on both cheeks. He turned back to Sir Kai and said, "I told you he would be here, didn't I? Welcome to court, Gawain! I have long wanted to meet you and offer you my friendship. Your father was a great man."

Gawain dropped to his knee and bowed his head. "My king," he began, "if it is an honour to be your nephew, it would be an even greater honour to be your knight. That is my sole desire."

"Ah," said the king, returning to his throne, "that is a different matter. Rise, Gawain, and tell me. Have you done any deeds worthy of a knight of the Round Table?"

"No, sire."

Terence could hardly believe his ears. "What about Sir Hautubris, milord?" he whispered loudly.

Immediately he knew he had made a terrible social error. Shocked faces turned toward him, and Terence realized that none of the other squires in the room had spoken a word. He blushed but kept his eyes level.

"And who are you, son?" the king asked him.

Terence gulped and said, "Terence, sir – Gawain's squire."

"I see," Arthur said. "Tell me about Sir Hautubris."

Gawain growled, "Terence!"

"No no, Gawain," Arthur said. "You must allow the king's word to take precedence. Continue, Squire Terence. Tell me about Sir Hautubris."

"Well," Terence stammered, "he was the knight who wanted to take our dinner – I mean me and milord and Trevisant – that's the Hermit of the Gentle Wood. I lived with him until milord came. And Sir Hautubris was angry because there wasn't any left. It was stew, sir," he explained.

"Go on," the king said, his eyes twinkling.

"So milord went out and told him we had just finished, but he was rude, so milord knocked him off his horse. So he got mad and tried to kill milord, and almost did, because milord didn't have any armour on—"

"You say that Gawain was wearing no armour?" the king interrupted.

"No sir, on account of being at dinner, I think," Terence said.

"Very proper," Arthur said, his lips twitching.

He looked at Gawain. "And was Sir Hautubris wearing armour, nephew?"

"Yes, sire."

Arthur turned back to Terence. "Go on," he said.

"So he tried to kill milord, like I said, but he couldn't because milord kept hitting him with the stewpot."

"With the what?" Sir Kai interrupted, a grin of delight spreading over his face.

"The stewpot, sir. Milord didn't have his sword, you see, so he hit Sir Hautubris in the head with the pot."

"Continue, please," said Arthur, suppressing a smile.

"That's almost everything. Milord took Sir Hautubris's sword away from him and said he wasn't to be trusted with it—" Terence heard Sir Kai snort, but he pressed on. "But then Sir Hautubris got another sword and tried to kill him from behind, so milord killed Sir Hautubris." Terence stopped, but no one spoke. "That's all," he added.

"Is this true, Gawain?" the king asked.

"In its essentials, sire," Gawain replied.

"This is not the first time that we have heard of Sir Hautubris," Arthur said. "Not so very long ago he inconvenienced one of my knights most severely."

Gawain looked astonished. "Sir Hautubris defeated one of your knights?"

A beautifully dressed knight, in yellow stockings, stepped forward and bowed before Gawain. "If it please your worship," he said, "I must thank you for relieving my sword from its oath to revenge itself upon that same villainous knight, that passing skilful knight of prowess who did dishonour on my person. I make no doubt you found him a very demon in battle, as did I, and I salute your escape from his wrath."

"Th-thank you, Sir . . . Sir . . ." Gawain said unsteadily.

Sir Kai coughed and said, "This is Sir Griflet, Gawain."

"Sir Griflet, then."

Sir Griflet bowed again and returned to his seat.

"In sum, then," the king said, "you fought an armed and armoured knight, yourself without armour or weapon—"

"No no, he had a stewpot," Sir Kai said.

"—and defeated him with his own sword," the king continued, ignoring his foster brother, "thus preserving an honoured religious man from persecution. It is a deed worthy of a knight of the Round Table." Gawain bowed his head but did not reply. The king smiled at Terence, and said, "You have a loyal squire."

"I have an ill-mannered squire," Gawain replied.

"Will you punish him for telling of this deed?"

Gawain hesitated, then shook his head. "No, sire. How could I punish him for telling what I wished to be known?"

The king burst into his clear, easy laughter and said, "Well spoken indeed! Kneel, Gawain."

Gawain knelt again, and the king drew the famous Sword Excalibur. He touched Gawain on each shoulder and on the top of his head and said, "Rise, Sir Gawain, and welcome to the Fellowship of the Round Table. Be ever true to your God; protect always your neighbour; honour always your king."

3

THE FIVE KINGS

The next morning, Terence went to war. With still an hour before dawn, he had dressed and was busy helping Gawain put on armour. When all the different plates were fastened in place and Terence saw his master in full armour for the first time, he gazed in wonder.

"You *do* look fine, milord!" he said in awe.

Gawain chuckled. "Just remember – I don't wear all this to look fine."

"I'll bet that's why Sir Griflet wears his."

"Likely," Gawain said. "But Terence?"

"Yes, milord?"

"Whether he does or doesn't, don't say so outside of this room. A squire never criticizes a knight, even if the knight is a fool."

"Yes, milord." Terence waited, but Gawain

did not move.

"One more thing, lad." Gawain handed Terence a small dagger in a black leather sheath. "No one should go to war without a weapon. This is yours."

Terence's eyes shone. The handle was intricately carved in the semblance of a winding serpent. He drew it from the sheath and peered fearfully at the long, wicked-looking blade. On impulse, Terence knelt at Gawain's feet and kissed his gauntlet.

"Nay, Terence," Gawain said. "Thank me by keeping it well and using it wisely. Now, let's go to war."

The war, they had discovered the night before, was against five rebel kings who refused to accept Arthur's right to rule. The King of Denmark, who controlled lands on the eastern coast of England, the King of Ireland, the King of the Vale, the King of Soleyse, and the King of the Isle of Longtains had joined into a formidable army and were marching toward Camelot. Most of the knights acted as if Arthur's army would defeat the Five Kings easily, but Arthur and Sir Kai had not joined in this confident talk.

As the marching column formed, Gawain and Terence took their assigned position at the rear, where they were joined by Tor, riding a powerful bay horse and wearing Sir Hautubris's armour, a gift from Gawain.

"Good morning, Tor!" Gawain called out cheerily.

"Good morning, Sir Gawain," Tor replied. "Hello, Terence."

"Good morning, sir," Terence said, pleased to be noticed. They trotted out of the castle, and Sir Ector's knights closed the gates behind them.

The day quickly grew hot and sultry, and the dust of the supply wagons in front of them formed a thick, gritty cloud that settled in every crease and corner. The knights rode with their visors down to filter out some of the dust, but Terence tasted grit all day. At midday the column stopped to eat a scanty meal and then was off again into the heat and dirt and sweat.

In mid-afternoon Sir Kai trotted back from the head of the column, his helm on his saddle. He watched for a moment, then fell into line alongside Gawain and mopped his brow with a damp rag he had tied to his wrist.

"Hello, Gawain," Sir Kai said.

"Hello, Sir Kai."

"Gawain. I've been wanting to talk to you."

"At your service," Gawain said. He raised the visor on his helm.

Sir Kai hesitated then grinned. "Did you really hit Sir Whoever with a stewpot?"

Gawain laughed. "It was all I had at hand."

Sir Kai chuckled. "I've suggested to Arthur that we should have a stewpot event at the next tournament. Better than bashing your friends off of horses with lances."

"Ay, but it would look silly," Gawain said. "No knight can endure looking silly."

"Oh, I wouldn't say that. Look at Griflet and Bagdemagus and that crew."

"Tell me about this Griflet," Gawain said. "Did he really lose a fight with Sir Hautubris?"

"Hautubris, was it? Never can remember these foreign names. Well, Griflet went out questing last month—"

"Went out what?"

"Questing. After the last wars, Arthur's knights got underfoot in the castle, so now he sends them out to look for adventures. He tells them to uphold the weak and so forth. Then, when they come back, they tell about their adventures. It gets them out of the king's hair for a space." Gawain grunted softly, and Kai added, "It's good for everyone. The knights like getting away now and again. I'd like it myself sometimes if I could."

"Why can't you?"

"I'm Arthur's seneschal. Someone has to see that everyone's fed and clothed."

"I guessed, but it seems a shame. I'd say that you're a fighter."

"I am," Sir Kai said agreeably. "Except for Arthur himself, I'm the best in Camelot. Or I was until you got here." Gawain said nothing, and Kai continued. "Anyway, Griflet came back from a quest last month with a story about a ferocious knight named – what was it? Hautubris – at a bridge, demanding to combat everyone who wanted to cross."

"Rabbit-brained thing to do," Gawain observed.

"Ay. Anyway, to hear Griflet tell it, they fought like men possessed for six hours until finally this Hautubris did something treacherous – I forget what – and villainously defeated him."

"Anyone else see it?"

"No."

"Then I wonder why Griflet didn't say he'd won."

Sir Kai laughed. "Hautubris took his horse and armour. Hard to explain that if he had won."

"Tell me, Kai," Gawain said, "how did this Griflet ever get knighted?"

"It wasn't Arthur's doing. When old Leodegrance gave Arthur the Round Table, it came with all of Leodegrance's knights. Some of them are proper chuckleheads, too. That was why Arthur started demanding some deed before he would knight anyone."

Gawain nodded, and they rode in silence for a few minutes. Sir Kai squinted for a moment into the sun, lowering to their right. "Cursed sun," he muttered. He looked back at Gawain and said, "You've a handful of brothers, haven't you?"

"Ay. There's Gaheris, Agrivain, and little Gareth. They plan to join me here someday."

"Fighters?"

"Not a bit of it. Gareth may be someday."

Sir Kai grunted and spat. "If they can't fight, they can stay where they are. Camelot's already crawling with tournament knights. If we win this war, it'll be because of Arthur and his peasant soldiers."

Terence eased himself in his saddle and wished for a drink and a rest. He checked the sun to see how long until sunset, and a flash of light in the distant woods caught his eye. He looked again, but there was nothing.

A rapid drumming of hooves came from behind. Tor, three or four places back in the column, had ridden up and joined Gawain and Sir Kai. Sir Kai looked at him sharply. "Who told you to break ranks, boy?"

"I'm sorry, Sir Kai, but I thought I should report," he said.

"Report what?" Sir Kai said, frowning.

"Signals, sir." He pointed at the hills to the right. "Someone up there."

"A flash of light?" Sir Kai asked. "I saw it. One flash of light doesn't make a signal."

"No, sir. There was a flash in reply – back there." Tor pointed directly behind them at the plain that they had just crossed.

Sir Kai squinted at the hills for a moment, then said, "It still could be nothing."

"Yes, sir," Tor replied.

"But you did right," Sir Kai muttered absently. "They couldn't be this close, already."

Gawain cleared his throat. "If you were going to attack this column, Kai, which direction would you come from?"

"From the west," he answered. "With the sun in my opponents' eyes."

"Or from behind?" Gawain said. "Or both?"

Sir Kai pondered this, then said, "You – Tor, is it? – go back to your place. I'll call you in a moment." Tor nodded and trotted back to the column. Sir Kai looked back at Gawain, "You any good in the woods?"

45

"All right, but I'm not what you need. Terence here is."

Sir Kai looked at Terence. "You a woodsman?"

"I . . . I grew up in the forest," Terence stammered.

"You'll come too, then," Sir Kai said. He galloped apart from the column, watched for a moment, then called out, "Scouting party forming here. Two knights, one squire! You!" he pointed at Tor. "And you!" this time at Gawain and Terence. "Fall out of line!"

Tor, Gawain, and Terence joined Sir Kai and waited until the column had passed. In a tight group, the four galloped across the plain toward the woods. As soon as they entered the forest, Terence began to feel at home. Instinctively he sorted out the various sounds in his mind. A squirrel chattered, and a hedgehog lumbered away from them.

"Now where?" Gawain asked Sir Kai.

"Up the hill, where the flashes were," he answered. They walked their horses up a slope, deeper into the forest, crashing through the thick brush. Terence no longer heard animal sounds.

"Milord?" Terence asked.

"Yes?" Gawain said.

"I could go faster on my own, milord. On foot, I

mean." Gawain frowned, and Terence added, "Quieter, too."

Gawain nodded and explained to Sir Kai what Terence wanted. Terence dropped lightly from his horse and slipped into the thickest part of the brush. In a few minutes, he began to hear animals again. A mole poked its nose up at his feet, and once Terence saw a doe with a wobbly fawn. The brush thinned, the trees grew more sparse, and the smell of the pines grew stronger. Without knowing why, Terence slowed. A faint rustling to his left drew his attention. A red fox was grinning at him from inside a holly bush. Terence grinned back. "Hello, Renard," he whispered.

"Hello yourself, Terence," the fox said.

For a second, Terence only stared. Then he backed cautiously away. The fox did not move; it only watched and panted and looked mischievous. "And where are you off to?" the fox asked. Terence swallowed and said nothing. "Well?" the fox asked again.

"I'm . . . nowhere. Going nowhere," Terence answered.

"Oh," the fox sounded disappointed. "And me thinking you were looking for that army on the next hill."

"Army?" Terence asked.

"Don't be a ninny, Terence," the fox said and began to change shape. It sprouted curly hair and two tiny horns and a pointed beard, and then out of the holly bush stepped the same little leafy figure that had chased Terence in his own forest the day he met Gawain. He grinned impishly and continued, "I'm here to help, you know."

"Who are you?" Terence stammered.

"Your friend, little though you may believe it. Look here." The green man squatted and began drawing in the dust. "We're here, and here's Gawain and the others. Right here – that's just over that hill – is the Five Kings' army. Your job is to break up that army."

"Me? By myself?"

"No, my lad. I'll be with you."

"But who are you? And how could I break up the army, anyway?"

"Trust me," the sprite said with an impish smile that did not inspire Terence with trust. "Here's what we'll do. You don't know it – in fact, only Arthur and Merlin know it – but the Five Kings do have a right to the throne. It's because of a ring, all inscribed with magic and such matters that simple peasant folk like you and me know nothing about." The little green man smiled innocently and continued. "The story is that whoever holds that ring may stand and declare his kingship over all England. The King of Longtains brought it to the alliance, and by that they make their claim against Arthur. Do you follow me?"

Terence blinked and thought for a moment. "I suppose so. But what can we do?"

"Steal the ring, lad."

"Steal it?"

"Of course. That's how Longtains got it. He took it from Uther Pendragon's treasury. So, no more talking. Let's go."

Ten minutes later, Terence and the little man crouched behind a mossy fallen tree and looked at the Five Kings' camp. "There," the green man said. "That tent in the middle, with the flag at the top. That's the kings' council tent, and there they keep the ring."

"Why don't they wear it?" Terence asked.

"They couldn't decide which one should have the honour. So they keep it in a jewelled box on the council table. Luck to you, lad." And then the little man was gone.

Terence hesitated, his mind in a whirl. He didn't know who his companion was, and he didn't trust him. One look at the little green leafy face was enough to be certain that the sprite loved mischief. But he had told the truth about the Five Kings' camp: here it was. Terence realized that he could not risk waiting. Taking a deep breath, he drew his new dagger from its sheath and slipped over the log into the camp. In a few steps he was at the council tent. Two knights strolled by him, but they paid him no mind. No one ever looked at servants and squires.

With his dagger, Terence cut a slit in the back of the tent, the glinting blade sliding through the rough canvas as if it were silk. Terence slipped through the hole, and though almost blind in the sudden gloom, he could see a jewelled box on a nearby table, just as the little man had promised. Quickly, Terence opened the box and removed the ring. Only then, his eyes adjusting to the shadows, did Terence realize he was not alone. Five bearded men dressed in rich purple and scarlet sat at a larger table a few feet away.

"Hey, put that back, boy," said one.

Terence's heart dropped and his stomach tightened. It was the Five Kings. With a gasp, he sprang backwards and dived through the hole he had cut in the tent. Shouts of "Hey! Who was that! What is he doing?" came from the tent, then "After him!"

Terence blundered into a knight, who cursed and aimed a kick at him, but Terence was already out of reach. He leaped around the maze of tents, hearing or imagining pursuit right behind him. Then he saw a row of horses, saddled and ready. Quickly he grabbed one, climbed into the saddle, and kicked it into a gallop. Only then did he look over his shoulder. No one followed. He rode into the cover of the woods and stopped, gasping for breath.

From a nearby oak came the chuckling voice of the little green man. "Right from under their noses, no less. I like a good thief, I do. But don't stop now, Terence. Here they come."

"There! In the trees!" came a shout, and then there was a rumble of horses. Terence kicked his horse into a run and held on for his life. Gawain had taught him to ride, but he had never had to ride at a dead run. Soon he had lost the reins, but he rode a war horse that was used to that. It probably thought it was leading a charge, and all Terence had to do was hold on to the saddle and duck under branches and brambles as they crashed through the forest. Twice he glanced behind him and saw five riders, growing nearer every second.

"Terence!" a voice shouted suddenly. It was Gawain. He and the others sat their horses on the far side of a little clearing. "Where did you get that horse?"

"The Five Kings!" Terence gasped. "Behind me!"

"With how many men?" Sir Kai asked sharply, but as he spoke the kings burst into the clearing behind Terence.

"I'll take the left," Sir Kai said abruptly and spurred his horse.

The next minute was a blur of motion to Terence. Sir Kai threw himself bodily against the king on the far left and swung his sword at the next one. Tor leaped from his own horse onto the middle king's horse, and brought him to the turf. Gawain had his fingers in one king's visor, shaking him back and forth, while he parried the sword of another and thrust. That king reeled and fell. Sir Kai lifted one king from his saddle and threw him against another.

"Ow! No biting!" Gawain shouted.

The king facing Tor swung at Tor's left, but with a move that Terence recognized easily, Tor leaped lightly to his right and chopped left-handed, and the king dropped. Immediately, Tor joined Sir Kai, who had just sent one king reeling backwards. In a moment, the other king lay sprawled at their feet. They turned toward Gawain, but Gawain had already dismounted and was wiping his sword on the grass.

"Are you hurt?" Sir Kai called to him.

Gawain looked resentfully at the body at his feet. "He bit my finger," he said.

"Sir Kai and Sir Gawain," King Arthur said, "I honour your courage, your skill and your loyalty. Even more, I thank you. You have won a great battle for my kingdom; all I have I owe to you." He kissed them on their cheeks and smiled warmly.

Terence was so proud of Gawain he thought he would burst. After the Five Kings had been killed, the planned ambush had never happened. As soon as Sir Kai had reported their victory to the king, Arthur had ridden alone up to the leaderless knights waiting in the forest, requested their surrender, and – having received it – sent them home unpunished, all swearing eternal allegiance to such a courageous and magnanimous king. Now, back at Camelot, Sir Kai and Gawain stood stiffly while their king thanked them formally. Terence beamed.

"Squire Terence?" the king said. Terence jumped with surprise. "For your part in this adventure, I also thank you. Will you do me the honour of accepting a small gift?" Terence gulped and nodded. Arthur took a thick yew longbow from a page and extended it to Terence. On his outstretched hand was the ring that Terence had taken from the kings. At Terence's request, Gawain had given it to the king privately. Arthur saw him look at the ring. His eyes glinted with a secret smile, but he continued, "This bow cannot be broken, nor can its string rot. Merlin says you still have to aim it, though."

"And now," the king continued, turning away from Terence, "where is Tor?"

"Here, your highness," Tor said, stepping forward.

"Kneel, Tor," Arthur said. Tor dropped at the king's feet. Arthur drew Excalibur from its scabbard and touched Tor on his shoulders and head. "Now rise, Sir Tor, and welcome to the Fellowship of the Round Table. Be ever true to your God; protect always your neighbour; honour always your king."

4

A HART, A HOUND
AND A VERY UGLY WOMAN

The wars were over. Only a few rebel knights and barons still resisted Arthur's authority, and these holdouts Arthur chose to ignore as insignificant. Instead, he turned his attention to being as skilful a leader in peace as he was in war. He established courts of justice and made laws restricting the taxes and forced labour that the lords often levied against peasants. The land knew peace for the first time that anyone could remember.

There was peace within the castle walls too, though Gawain called it tedium. Every day was a leisurely round of feasting and telling tales and dallying with fair ladies. Gawain devoted much time to the ladies, all of whom seemed to find him irresistible. He soon acquired the reputation of being a ladies' favourite, but to Terence it seemed that Gawain preferred his evenings spent drinking and arguing with other knights. The king and Sir Kai and the king's judges stayed busy, but the knights were left to amuse themselves. Even Terence, who as a squire actually had a few daily tasks to perform, had more time than he knew how to fill.

A squire, Terence learned, was a sort of in-between person. His position was too low for the knights to notice him, but at the same time too lofty for him to be welcome among the servants. He wasn't even at home among the other squires. They all dreamed of becoming knights themselves, and all their talk was about the great knightly deeds they would perform. Terence had no such ambitions. Only around Gawain and Tor did he feel at ease.

One other person in the court did show an interest in Terence. One day in a corridor, Merlin stopped him. "Squire Terence, isn't it?" he asked.

"Yes, sir?" Terence said, a bit apprehensively.

"Ah, good," the old man said. "Tell me, how is my old friend Trevisant? I knew that he had taken in a boy to raise."

"He was well when I left him, sir."

"He's a great man," Merlin said simply. "But

that's why you were left with him." Merlin looked hard at Terence's eyes for a long, uncomfortable minute, then the enchanter nodded and smiled. "I am glad you've come to court," he said. "But I don't choose to tell you why."

"Thank . . . thank you, sir," Terence said, bewildered. Merlin chuckled and continued on his way.

Terence filled his days practising with his new longbow until his arms ached and then practising his horsemanship until other parts did. It was a pleasant life in many ways, but he chafed for lack of occupation. So he was relieved when this tranquil (or tedious) existence was disturbed by the announcement one fine June day that the king was to be married. Sir Leodegrance, who had given the Round Table to Arthur, was now giving the king his daughter, Guinevere. All the ladies of the court, as well as Sir Griflet and many of the other knights, were in an uproar, ordering new clothes and designing new ways of dressing their hair for the wedding feast, which was to last seven days and end with a tournament. Visiting barons and nobles began to arrive, bearing their wedding gifts and all planning to stay for the feast. Sir Kai, drinking a vast amount of wine with Gawain and Tor and a few others in Gawain's chambers one night, complained that it was easier to provision for a war than for a wedding, but even Sir Kai admitted that the king's wedding must be splendid.

And splendid it was. All of the lords and ladies wore glittering clothes, so the royal Chapel of St Stephen was afire with colour. Most brilliant of all was young Guinevere, in a shimmering ivory robe with a rich blue underdress and trim, all interwoven with cloth of gold. When she and Arthur kissed, ladies wept and men cheered.

The feasting began directly after the wedding. Arthur had tables set for hundreds in his great banquet hall. He and Guinevere sat at a shorter table at the head of the hall, and the guests sat at two long rows of tables that ran along each side. In the centre of the hall, between the two rows of tables, servants scurried back and forth, carrying roast venison and oxen and boar and platters piled high with poultry and trenchers filled with hot and cold soups and plates of custards and calf's-foot jellies and pastries and stoup after stoup of ale and wine. Terence stood correctly behind Gawain's chair at one of the long tables.

At midnight of the first night's feast, just as Terence was losing interest in the spectacle and beginning to wish for bed, adventure arrived. From the kitchen came a terrific crash, followed by the sound of a woman in hysterics. More crashes followed, and then the kitchen door burst open. Into the banquet hall bounded a gigantic hart, pure white except for his hooves, eyes, and majestic antlers. It raced down the centre of the room, directly toward Arthur. Servants threw down their plates of food and dived under tables. The stag stopped in front of Arthur, then sprang onto the king's table and began running again. Food and wine flew willy-nilly onto the floor and the clothes of the guests.

At that moment, a monstrous deerhound, as white as the hart itself, burst in from the kitchen, baying loudly. Seeing the hart, it leaped onto the table and gave chase. Ladies screamed, and men bellowed vague commands that no one heeded – "Stop that!" and "Somebody do something!" Terence saw Tor wiping soup from his face, and he heard Sir Griflet scream in an outraged voice, "Look what they've done to my hat!" Two knights whom Terence did not know joined the chase, swinging their swords recklessly and ineffectively. The hart's antlers knocked a chandelier, and shadows from the candles veered crazily back and forth.

Finally the hart gave a mighty bound and disappeared through an open window into the night. Like a flash, the hound followed it, and then all was quiet in the banquet hall except for Sir Griflet muttering wrathfully over his hat. The king stood, smiling slightly.

"I do hope all of you had eaten your fill before the excitement began," he said. "As tonight's dinner appears to be concluded, let us repair to our rooms and trust that tomorrow's feast will be less eventful."

The guests seemed to relax again. Servants and ladies and one or two knights crawled out from under the tables, and a low murmur of conversation began. In the hubbub, a voice called out, "Just a moment, please." It was Merlin. "I don't think we're done with this business," he said. "Listen!"

At first Terence heard nothing, but then, through the open kitchen door, came a slow clop-clop-clopping. In a moment, a massive white mule appeared in the open doorway. On the mule's back was a slender, heavily veiled woman, dressed all in white. She stooped slightly as the mule went through the doorway, and then sat in silence until the mule had walked deliberately the length of the hall and stopped in front of the king's table. A hush fell over the hall. Something he had never felt before stirred in Terence's heart, and he felt at once horrified by the woman and drawn to her.

"Shame!" the woman said suddenly in a rich, low voice. Terence's heart leaped at the sound. "Shame to you, King Arthur, and to all of your vaunted knights."

"Madam," King Arthur said. "For what cause do you say so?"

"Has any of you ever seen such a hart or brachet as those that were just here?" she asked, her gorgeous voice rising and filling the room with warmth.

Terence leaned close to Gawain and whispered, "What's a brachet?"

"Female hound," Gawain answered shortly in a strained voice. Gawain's eyes had not left the woman since she entered the room.

"And yet, when these beasts enter your banquet hall, all you can say is that you hope it does not happen again," the woman continued. "For shame that you should leave these adventures so lightly!"

For a moment no one spoke. Then Gawain vaulted lightly over the table and walked up to the mule, looking piercingly at the woman's veil. "A battle I call an adventure," he said. "A dragon in the woods is an adventure. But how is a hart and hound, even oddly coloured ones, an adventure?"

The woman looked at Gawain silently for a moment, then nodded. "The greatest adventures begin simply," she said. Again, her voice was low, but it throbbed richly and filled the room. Then she gestured at the room that lay in shambles around them. "But do you consider this simple?"

"It is a nuisance, indeed, but no adventure," Gawain replied.

"Nephew," the king said gently, "let us hear the lady."

"I beg your pardon, sire," he said. "But we have yet to see whether this visitor is indeed a lady. A man may wear a veil." He looked intently at the woman and said, "Show us your face, madam."

Every eye turned toward the woman, but she did not answer. Deliberately, she lifted her veil over her head. For a second there was a stunned silence, and then one of Guinevere's ladies uttered a tiny squawk and fainted. A man swore, and several knights crossed themselves surreptitiously.

The woman on the mule was the ugliest woman Terence had ever seen. Her nose was impossibly long and crooked. Her eyes squinted. Her thin, almost invisible lips opened to reveal a loose scattering of yellow, carious teeth. Her upper lip was dark and bristly, and from a huge black mole on her neck grew a thick tuft of hair. Her cheeks were deeply scarred, as if by pox. Aghast, Terence looked away. Others, too, averted their eyes. Only Arthur, Merlin, and Gawain looked steadily at the woman's features. Arthur and Merlin's faces were expressionless, but Gawain looked stricken.

"Do you believe now that I am a woman?" she said.

Gawain bowed. "I do not doubt you, madam. But I still see no adventure in a stag and a hound." His voice was harsher than before.

"Those who choose to avoid danger make it a point not to see adventures, I believe." The woman's voice, too, had changed. Now there was a mocking note.

"And those who are fools see adventures where there are none," Gawain retorted. As if realizing his rudeness, Gawain bowed again and added, "Meaning no offence, of course, madam."

The woman smiled without humour and said, "Offence taken all the same, young coxcomb."

"As you wish," Gawain said, his jaw clamped shut.

"I had heard," the woman said to Arthur,

keeping an eye on Gawain at the same time, "that your court was the most gallant of all courts, and the most respectful. I see now that that was nonsense. But are there knights here willing to dare an adventure?"

"Sir Gawain appears to have forgotten himself," Arthur agreed. "But he himself will dare—"

"Sir Gawain?" the woman interrupted. "Do you mean to tell me that this pompous, self-absorbed fribble is Sir Gawain! Appalling! I had heard he was the best knight in the court." She looked into Gawain's eyes, and the mocking note in her voice grew stronger. "I do hope that Camelot isn't attacked by a band of blind, crippled old women. But perhaps you have other knights who could protect Sir Gawain from them."

Gawain met her gaze, and his eyes flashed, but he said nothing. At last, Arthur said quietly, "What would you have us do, my lady?"

"You must send two knights out on the adventure," the woman said. "One to follow the hound and one to follow the hart."

Merlin spoke suddenly. "Do as she says, your highness."

"Sir Tor!" Arthur called. "You will follow the hound."

"King Arthur," the woman said. "Send Sir

64

Gawain after the hart." She looked at him from the corner of her eye. "Perhaps he will find adventure where he saw none before."

"So be it," said the king.

The mule turned slowly and started toward the kitchen door. As she passed by Gawain, the woman whispered, "Fribble!"

"Harridan!" Gawain replied promptly. And his eyes followed her until she had disappeared.

5

QUESTING

By noon the next day, Terence, Gawain, and Tor were twenty miles from Camelot, pressing deeper into the forest. It had not been a pleasant ride. Gawain had been broodingly silent all morning, and neither Tor nor Terence wanted to interrupt his preoccupation. Instead, they had busied themselves with the hunt and with controlling the greyhounds that the king had lent them for the chase.

Tor finally broke the silence. "Shall we stop here for a luncheon?" he asked. Gawain did not reply. Tor looked at Terence and shrugged. "I said, shall we—"

"The sooner we catch those animals, the sooner we'll be done with this fool's errand," Gawain said gruffly. "Let's press on."

"I'm hungry," Tor replied simply. "I'm stopping."

"Suit yourself. We're not," Gawain said, trotting ahead.

Terence had been thinking longingly about his lunch for over an hour, but he took a deep breath and resigned himself. Tor grinned at Terence, understanding in his eyes, and tossed him a half loaf of bread. Terence smiled gratefully and booted his horse after Gawain.

Terence's horse gave out at about three. Terence had never seen an exhausted horse before and did not recognize the signs until the animal stumbled and fell. Gawain dismounted and impatiently examined the horse.

"Why didn't you tell me your horse was in this state?" he demanded. Terence quailed at the anger in Gawain's eyes. "Couldn't you hear him gasping? Couldn't you feel him shaking? There's nothing worse than someone who does that to an animal." Gawain glowered at the horse for a moment, then snapped at Terence, "Well? Start getting camp ready. You can do that well enough, anyway." Smarting with a helpless sense of injustice, Terence began making camp.

An hour later, Tor joined them. He glanced at Terence's horse, then dismounted. "Had to rest the horse, hey?" he remarked.

"That's right," Gawain grumbled. "We're lucky Terence didn't kill it."

Tor stopped in his tracks. "Well of all the conceited – you don't mean you've blamed Terence for it?"

"Who else?" Gawain frowned.

"You, you stupid sod! Who was it who wouldn't stop and rest? Who was it who set the pace? As if any horse could keep up with your Guingalet!"

Gawain flushed, but he answered, "He could have told me his horse was in trouble."

Tor laughed shortly. "You mean during the delightful conversation that the two of you were holding. So cheerful and chatty as you've been today!"

Gawain glowered at him. "I only wanted to get this pointless chase done with."

Tor frowned at Gawain for a moment, then said, "Look, Gawain. I don't know who's put you so out of sorts, but it wasn't Terence."

For a long moment, Gawain looked at the ground. Then he raised his eyes. "You're right, Tor. I'm sorry, Terence. Forgive me my ill temper?"

Terence gulped. "Yes, milord."

Later, after they had eaten, Tor leaned against a

log and said to Gawain, "Do you want to tell us what's bothering you?"

Gawain shrugged. "I told you. I just think we're wasting our time."

"Maybe," Tor agreed. "But I don't mind getting away from court. Getting tired of doing the pretty to all the courtiers and ladies. I thought you were, too."

Gawain thought for a minute, then said, "Well, I was. But I'd just as soon be off to do something worth my bother."

"It might be. You must admit, the animals were unnatural. And as for that lady on the mule—"

"Her!" Gawain snorted. "That was no lady! What was Arthur thinking, sending off two knights just because an old hag says to!"

Tor raised his eyebrows and said, "Oh she was a hag, certainly, but I wouldn't call her old. Her voice was young enough." Gawain nodded reflectively, but he said nothing. Tor continued, "Do you think she was an enchantress?"

Gawain laughed harshly. "Never. The first thing an enchantress learns is how to make herself beautiful. I've never known one who wouldn't take your breath away to look at her."

Tor looked surprised. "Have you known so many enchantresses, then?"

Gawain nodded, but something forbidding clouded his face, and Tor asked no other questions.

The next day was better. Gawain was still poor company, but he guarded his tongue and his temper. Shortly after noon, the greyhounds picked up a scent, and the hunt began in earnest. Two hours later, the three came to an open field where two knights in full armour were fighting.

"Take this, thou varlet!" one of the knights cried, putting all his strength into an overhead chop. The other knight parried the blow with his sword and managed to deflect it somewhat, but it still bit into his armour at the shoulder. Blood welled from the gash.

"By Jove, you've got a good swing there," the wounded knight cried. "I'm sure you'll have me in a few minutes."

"Not at all," the other said. "Not while you display such brilliant defence. I'm sure *I* could never have parried that blow."

"Oh, but see, you've opened up that wound in my shoulder," the first knight replied. "I'll surely bleed to death soon."

"Oh dear," the other said. "And it was just healed over, too."

"Never mind. Shall we go on?"

"Of course. Die, miscreant!"

Gawain's solemn lips relaxed slightly, and he trotted Guingalet up to the combatants. "I beg your pardon," he said. "I hope I'm not interrupting anything."

"Well, actually," the wounded one said, "you are, a bit."

"Now Brian," said the other, "there's no call to be rude."

"I don't see that," he replied. "After all, he asked. In fact, if you ask me, he's the one who was rude. It should be clear that we're busy."

Gawain cleared his throat. "Very true, Sir Knight. But if you'll excuse my vulgar curiosity, what have I interrupted?"

The two knights stiffened, and the wounded one said, "I fail to see how that's any of your affair."

"Quite right," the other agreed.

Gawain nodded understandingly, and said, "You are right that I am an outsider. But as an impartial observer, perhaps I can mediate your disagreement. Surely you two do not really wish to kill each other." He dismounted and stood near the two knights.

"No, no, of course not," said the wounded knight. "But what is a man of honour to do in the face of such insults? One cannot show weakness."

"Exactly," agreed the other. "To seek mediation would be cowardly."

"What insults?" Gawain pursued.

The two hesitated and looked at each other. After a moment, the wounded one said, "Did I call you a recreant knight? Or did you call me one?"

"You called me craven, I know."

"Was that before or after you called me a scurrilous knave?"

"Before, I'm sure."

"What about varlet? I'm sure you called me a varlet."

"And so you are! Blackguard!"

"I – a blackguard? Nay, 'tis thou that art a blackguard!"

The two knights raised their swords again, but Gawain stepped between them. "But what began all the insults?" he asked.

Again, the two knights looked at each other and thought for a while. "It wasn't a woman, I know," one of them said at last.

"No, no. Silly to fight about a woman," the other agreed. "Do you owe me money?"

"No, it isn't money either. I'm sure it will come to me. Did you insult my mother?"

"Of course not. She's my mother too, after all."

"What, do you mean to tell me you're brothers?"

Gawain demanded.

"Good heavens, where are our manners? My name is Sorlouse of the Forest, and this is my brother Brian of the Forest." Both knights bowed correctly.

"You're a couple of prize loobies," Gawain said. "Shame on you!"

The brothers looked at each other for a moment, then they raised their swords together and turned on Gawain. "I take such insults from no man!" declared Sorlouse.

"Nor do I!" added Brian. "Unsheath thy sword, varlet!"

"No," Gawain said.

The brothers looked at each other. "Art thou craven?" asked Sorlouse. Gawain shrugged, and Sorlouse continued, "Recreant knight! Thou miscreant!"

"Scurrilous knave," added his brother. "And . . . and . . ."

"Blackguard," Gawain supplied.

"Blackguard. Thank you," Brian said.

"I still won't fight you," said Gawain. "I'm busy."

"You weren't too busy to interfere in our affairs," Sorlouse snapped.

"I beg your pardon, of course, but I wanted to

ask you if you had seen a white stag, followed by a white brachet, pass this way."

"That's it!" the brothers said together. "We were fighting over who should gain glory by pursuing the white hart!" Brian explained.

"Which way did it go?" Gawain asked. The brothers pointed due north, and Gawain waved his arm to Tor and Terence, saying, "Come on."

As they rode past the two knights, one of them said, "But what about us, then?"

"Find something else to fight about," Gawain called over his shoulder.

As they entered the forest on the other side of the clearing, Terence heard one of the brothers say, "Are you sure you don't owe me money?"

Gawain's face was less severe as they rode away from Sorlouse and Brian, and when, a few minutes later, Tor rode alongside him and whispered, "Varlet," he smiled for the first time in two days.

"Heaven preserve us from the witless," Gawain said, shaking his head.

"One thing bothers me," Tor said. "They mentioned the hart, but they said nothing about the hound. I hope they haven't been separated."

"I didn't think of that," Gawain said. "Do you want to go back and ask?"

"No. It wouldn't do any good. If they *have* been separated, I'd still have to follow the hart and hope the hound is near."

They saw the hart less than an hour later. It was feeding quietly in a meadow, and the white hound was nowhere in sight. Tor muttered an oath, then called out, "Luck, Gawain! Here's where we separate!" while Gawain and Terence let the greyhounds loose and galloped after them. The hart bounded away through the thickest part of the woods, with hounds and horses hot at his heels. Terence's mount fell behind Guingalet and the hounds, but it was easy to follow the greyhounds' baying. Then there were voices.

Pushing through a mesh of brambles, Terence came upon a river. Near him, Gawain sat on Guingalet; on the other side of the river sat a strange knight on a white horse. Gawain shouted at the knight in an exasperated tone, "Are you off your head?"

"I know not as for that, sir knight, but I tell you again, no knight shall pass this river but if they shalt joust with me," the strange knight called back.

"Why not?" Gawain demanded.

"I am Alardin of the Hill, guardian of this river."

"Guardian from what? You think I'm going to

spit in it?"

"Nor you nor any other knight shall cross without having to do with me," Alardin of the Hill replied.

"Haven't you anything better to do with your time?" Gawain demanded.

"Nor you nor any knight—"

"I know, I know," Gawain shouted. "All right, here I come. I'll fight you, if you're so set on it." In a minute he and Terence sat their dripping horses on the other bank.

"Now we shall joust," Alardin said with satisfaction.

"With what?" Gawain asked. "I don't have a. lance with me."

"I shall provide you a lance, sir knight," Alardin said. He rode into the woods and returned in a few seconds, carrying a lance. He gave Gawain the lance and said, "We shall charge from those two markers." He pointed at two little flags on opposite ends of a small field along the river. Gawain shook his head but rode to his place.

"Now!" Alardin shouted, and the knights rode toward each other. Gawain's lance seemed to waver once, then lightly tapped Alardin's lance to one side a split second before hitting Alardin on the breastplate. There was a terrific thump, and both horses reared. When they came down, the two knights were still on their horses. Alardin still held his lance, which had missed Gawain by several inches, but Gawain only held the butt of his. The rest lay in a hundred fragments on the field around them.

"What was this made of?" Gawain demanded wrathfully. "Cork?"

Alardin raised his visor and looked at Gawain, surprise and growing anger in his face. "We shall joust again!" he snapped, wheeling his horse and galloping back to his marker.

"Are you going to give me another lance?" Gawain called.

"You've had your lance, and you wasted it!" Alardin shouted and charged.

Gawain swore and drew his sword. He uttered a quick syllable to Guingalet, who danced lightly across Alardin's path. Alardin, holding his lance in his right hand, shifted his aim so that the lance pointed across his body, but Gawain was already on him. Gawain grabbed the lance behind the point and the forward motion of the horses swept both knights from their saddles. Alardin's horse tumbled in a heap, tried to rise, then fell back on its side, its leg broken.

"You cur!" Gawain shouted furiously, struggling

to his feet. "Now get up!"

Alardin struggled to a kneeling position and bowed his head. "I yield myself to your honour," he said.

Gawain cursed him fervently. "You'll do no such thing! You wanted to fight, now fight. You've just destroyed a beautiful animal with your game. Get up!"

"Sir knight—" Alardin began. Gawain kicked him back onto his rump. After a second of surprise, he clanked stiffly to his feet and drew his sword, crying, "For that, you shall pay!"

Gawain killed him, his sword biting deeply into Alardin's helm. "*Salaud!*" Gawain muttered. Removing his own helm, he walked to Alardin's writhing horse. He caught the horse's head and held it, crooning something soothing in a language that Terence did not know until the horse quieted. Then Gawain's sword flashed again, and the horse lay dead at his feet. He climbed back on Guingalet, and grimly pointed north. "That way."

They no longer heard the greyhounds, who had stayed close to the hart, but Gawain did not waver from his northerly course. In a very few minutes they came to a solitary castle in the midst of the forest. The drawbridge was down, and Terence could hear hounds yelping inside. Without hesitation, they galloped across the drawbridge into the central court, where the hart was already dead, and the hounds were worrying its bleeding carcass. As they arrived, a stout knight in full armour burst into the courtyard. He saw the dead hart, and with a choking cry whipped out his sword and attacked the greyhounds. His sword flashed right and left, and in seconds five greyhounds were stretched dead around the hart, and the last one was crawling away, whimpering and dragging an almost severed hind leg behind it. Gawain leaped from his horse and with one merciful blow killed the wounded dog. Then he turned very slowly to face the knight.

"What the devil did you do that for?" he asked in a dangerously calm voice.

"That hart was a pet, given me by my lady," the knight responded.

"But why kill the dogs?" Gawain said. "They were only doing what they were bred to do. If you want revenge, attack the hunter."

"Are you the hunter?" the knight asked.

"I am."

The knight said no more. He lifted his sword high and ran at Gawain, chopping down at him with all his might. Gawain deflected the blow and gave the knight a glancing blow on his left side that sent him staggering. Gawain followed up this blow with a flashing chop into his right side. The knight reeled away, almost going to his knees.

"A blow for every dog you killed," Gawain said deliberately. Again he struck the knight on the left, then on the right. The knight fell but struggled back up. Gawain let him get to his knees then knocked him down again. Again Gawain waited for the knight to get up, then said, "And one more blow for the hound you made *me* kill." He lifted his sword again, and Terence looked away.

But no crash and sickly thump of decapitated head or mutilated body came to Terence's ears. Instead, a high-pitched, whining wail echoed around the castle, and Terence looked back. A lady in a scarlet gown had appeared and had thrown herself on the knight. Gawain still held his sword over his head, but could not strike without hitting the lady.

"Spare him, O knight," the lady shrieked, weeping. "Without my lord, my own life would be empty and meaningless. My love is my whole life." She sobbed convulsively, and tears ran in streams down her puckered face.

"Oh, all right," Gawain said, lowering his sword. "I'll spare him if you'll stop crying."

"Oh sir! You are the flower of chivalry, the fairest

of knights, knowing well that no virtue becomes a knight so well as mercy, I honour you and your noble parents—" the woman cried, without abating her sobs.

"Yes yes, that's fine. You needn't be mawkish about it," Gawain said hastily. The battered knight climbed to his feet behind his lady and stood unsteadily for a moment. Then, still holding his lady in front of him, he reached out with his sword and tried to hit Gawain again. Gawain knocked the blow down without difficulty, and the knight stepped back, pulling his still weeping lady after him, using her as a shield.

"You *are* contemptible!" Gawain said incredulously. He feinted quickly to his right. When the knight shifted his weeping shield that way, Gawain pivoted the other way and smashed his sword down on the knight's foot. The knight howled with pain and let go of the lady. Gawain shoved her roughly away from her lord. The knight recovered and swung at Gawain, but Gawain dodged and swung a mighty blow at neck level. Before the blow could land, though, the lady threw herself in front of the knight again. Gawain could not check his blow, and the lady's head rolled between Gawain and the knight.

For a long minute the two knights stared at it in

eerie silence. Then the knight fell to his knees and clasped the lady's body.

"Kill me," he whispered at last.

"No," Gawain said hoarsely. "Death would be too gentle. You may bury your lady's body, but you will carry her head – and the hart's – to Camelot and tell King Arthur your story, how you used your wife for a shield and shamed us both for the rest of our lives. If you fail to do this, I will hunt you down and kill you by inches. Understand?"

The knight nodded.

"What is your name?" Gawain asked.

"Sir Ablamor of the Marsh," the knight said. "And her name was—"

"No!" Gawain shouted. "I don't want to know! Tell the king that Sir Gawain sent you. Now go!"

Gawain remounted Guingalet, and without looking at Terence rode slowly back across the drawbridge, out of the castle. Silently Terence followed.

"Milord?" he said, when he caught up. "It wasn't your fault."

Gawain shook his head, and there was nothing else to say.

Two hours later they found Tor in an open field, arguing hotly with a lady. At Tor's feet knelt a knight, and the white hound sat on her haunches next to Tor's horse. On the other side of Tor's horse a dwarf sat on a beautiful black mare, aloofly watching the argument.

"Madam, I tell you, he's already yielded to me," Tor said.

"What difference does that make?" the lady demanded. "This is Sir Abelleus!"

"Well, good for him," Tor said impatiently. "And who is Sir Abelleus?"

"The falsest knight ever to ride a horse," the lady exclaimed in trilling accents. "He killed my brother before mine own eyes," she announced. "And he but livest to strike down good knights."

"Maybe this will teach him not to strike down any more," Tor said. He looked at the kneeling Abelleus. "Do you promise not to be so naughty any more and to stop striking down good knights?"

"Oh yes," Abelleus said, nodding emphatically.

"And do you agree to let me take this hound back to the court without interfering with me any more?"

"Yes sir. Beg your pardon for bothering you, sir."

"And do you apologize for killing this lady's brother?"

"Oh yes. Very sorry, madam."

"Right then. What reparation should he pay you,

do you think?" Tor asked the lady.

"I've told you!" she said, waving her arms dramatically. "He must pay with his life."

"How about all of his lands? Do you have any lands?" Tor asked the knight.

"I have a castle in Winchelsea," he answered. "But it needs work."

"How about a run-down castle in Winchelsea?" Tor asked the lady.

"Never!" she pronounced.

"Not really run-down. As soon as the roof's repaired it will really be very nice," Abelleus contributed.

"Abelleus will even pay for the repair, won't you?" Tor added. Abelleus nodded vigorously.

"I shall never rest so long as we both live," the lady cried.

The dwarf snorted and spoke for the first time. "Well then, that solves our problem, Sir Tor. Kill the lady."

"I can't kill a lady, Plogrun," Tor protested.

"Would you like me to?" Abelleus asked eagerly.

"Oh, do be quiet," Tor said. By this time Gawain and Terence had joined the group. Tor turned to them and said, "Hello, Gawain. Terence."

"Tor," Gawain replied.

"This is Plogrun," Tor said. "He's my squire. I

84

picked him up earlier. He was serving a couple of real stinkers, who challenged me. I defeated them, and he said he'd prefer to follow me. I think he'll work out fine. Plogrun, this is Sir Gawain and his squire Terence."

"I am honoured, sir," Plogrun said, bowing as deeply as a dwarf can bow. "Pleased to meet you, Terence."

"Hello," Terence said.

"Look here," Abelleus said. "I don't mean to interrupt, but—"

Gawain said, "Oh don't let us disturb you, Tor. You were just saying that you couldn't kill a lady." Gawain smiled, but only with his lips.

"I don't see what's so difficult about it," the dwarf commented.

"Nothing at all," Abelleus said. "Really, they're much easier than men."

Tor looked at him contemptuously. "I'm beginning to think I ought to kill you after all."

"I told you!" the lady said.

"But I've already yielded," Abelleus pointed out.

Gawain interrupted, "Look here, Tor. If it bothers you to kill a lady, you could let someone else do it."

"An excellent notion," the dwarf said approvingly.

Suddenly, Tor's lips twitched, and he said, "That would be all right, I suppose."

"You would allow this villain to kill me?" the lady asked Tor. Her eyes were as round as coins. "How could you bear such a piteous sight?"

"I'd look away," Tor explained.

"Why?" Abelleus asked.

Ignoring him, Tor said, "Unless you're willing to accept Abelleus's reparations, of course."

The woman clasped both hands to her breast and moaned, "Ah, that a fair lady should be so abused." Suddenly, she pulled a dagger from her robe and threw herself at Abelleus. Abelleus caught her arm easily and plucked the dagger from her hand. He raised his arm to drive the dagger into the woman's heart, and Tor cut off his head.

Tor swore. The lady grasped Abelleus's head and raised it triumphantly from the ground. "There! There! Long have I dreamed of holding thee so!"

"Well, I hope you like it," Tor said angrily, driving his sword into the dirt at her feet. "Because you're going to see a lot of it. Toss me some cord, Plogrun." Tor took the rope and deftly secured Abelleus's head to it with a bewildering variety of knots. Then he tied it roughly around the lady's neck.

"You may remove this head only at Camelot.

There is a . . . a spell on the cord, and if you try to cut it or untie it before then, your . . . your nose will grow to three times its normal size. Now, go! And take this brachet with you," Tor added, handing the hound's leash to the lady. "When you reach Arthur's court, you will tell him of your cruelty and deliver this hound with Sir Tor's compliments. Now go!" The woman tottered away, her enemy's head bouncing and dripping blood on her gown.

"A magic cord?" Gawain asked after a minute.

Tor grinned. "She seemed easy to fool. After all, she believed you when you pretended that you could kill a woman."

Gawain and Terence looked at each other, but neither spoke.

6

MARHAULT AND MORGAN

The two knights and two squires rode eastward along a meandering forest trail. Tor rode ahead with Gawain, telling his story. Tor had won three fights in the few hours since they parted, and he was clearly pleased with himself. In his excitement, he did not seem to notice that Gawain said nothing of his own adventures.

Terence rode alongside the dwarf Plogrun, but although he could not resist peeking at him every now and then, he was too shy to speak to the strange squire. Finally, Plogrun broke the silence.

"Your name's Terence?" he asked politely.

"Yes, sir," Terence said.

"Don't call me sir. A squire shows respect to every knight and every lady, but never to another squire."

"Sorry," Terence stammered.

"There, see? You've just done it again," the dwarf pointed out. "Don't apologize either."

Terence started to say he was sorry again, but caught himself.

"Good." Plogrun nodded. "You can't ride worth a farthing, so you must be a new squire."

"None of your business!" Terence snapped.

"Even better," the dwarf said approvingly. "Nothing to be ashamed of, being new. You've a good master, too. A squire is only as good as his knight. Now me, I'm the best squire there is, but I've had the worst luck with masters, let me tell you. I can't say what a relief it is to finally squire a knight with as much potential as Sir Tor. Not a good knight yet, of course. Only beat Abelleus by sheer luck, actually, but I've seldom seen a young knight show more potential."

When they had ridden through the forest in silence for another hour, Gawain and Tor pulled up at the edge of a long, grassy clearing. A stream ran along one side of the meadow, and Terence saw a trout jump.

"Terence! You cook trout?" Gawain called.

"My specialty, milord," Terence responded eagerly.

"We'll stop here for the night, then," Gawain

89

said. "I'll tend to your horse, Terence. You go catch some fish."

"An *excellent* master," Plogrun muttered as Terence leaped to the ground and started toward the stream.

The water was fresh and cool, the stream teemed with fish, and the trees along the eastern bank were thick and shady. Terence quickly fashioned a hook and line, captured a pocketful of plump insects for bait, and settled himself comfortably on the bank. Nothing could have been more blissfully relaxed. The others set up camp about thirty yards away, by a pair of drooping willows. Before long they joined him.

"Good fishing, Terence?" Tor asked. Terence grinned and gestured at a pile of fish behind him.

Gawain squatted next to Terence. "Don't fish the stream out today, Terence. We may stay here for a while."

"My horse?" Terence asked quickly.

"Ay. We rode it too hard today after yesterday's mauling. It'll be better after a few days' rest, I hope."

Tor grinned and sat next to Gawain. "I'm in no hurry to get back to court anyway. More pleasant here."

"And it seems to me," Plogrun added pensively, "that this long meadow here might be made for a bit of jousting practice."

"Do you need jousting practice, Plogrun?" Tor said, grinning.

"No, sir. Beggin' your pardon, but I thought this might be a good time for you to learn how to brace your lance with your armour and not your body, since it was only by the grace of God that you didn't break your elbow, wrist and all your ribs – and not just your lance – in the fight with Abelleus," Plogrun said woodenly. "Meanin' no offence, of course."

Gawain gave a shout of laughter. Tor reddened but smiled crookedly.

"Hush," Terence said. "I've got a bite."

That began an idyllic two weeks of jousting and jesting and education. Plogrun taught Terence how to split a stout ash and shape it into a lance. Together they made eleven blunt practice lances – which, with a sharpened one that Tor had taken from Plogrun's former masters, made an even dozen – while Gawain and Tor sparred with swords in the clearing. Terence showed Plogrun, who had been astonished at Terence's way with trout, a few cooking tricks, and Plogrun, a skilled archer, gave Terence lessons with his bow.

As soon as the new lances had cured in the sun,

Gawain and Tor began to joust. This practice was much harder on Tor than on Gawain, but Tor bore his lumps with determined good humour. Plogrun would watch each pass critically and then, after his new master had hit the turf, would join Gawain in giving Tor advice and criticism. Even through this, Tor resolutely maintained his smile.

After a few days, Terence began to notice something odd. The knights would practise all morning and then rest at noon, but whereas Tor would collapse in the shade, exhausted, Gawain seemed as fresh or even fresher than when they began. Only in the evening would he seem to grow tired. Terence spoke of this one evening, when Tor and Plogrun were out of earshot. Gawain looked startled, but after a moment, he said, "Ay, lad. You're right. At noon I feel I could fight an army." They looked at each other for a minute, and then Gawain said, "It's your hermit's gift, isn't it? That my strength would rise with the sun. I've not given it a thought since that day."

Some days, Terence grew bored with the jousting and slipped off to the forest to practise archery or to gather herbs. One fine warm day he came across a fresh deer track. The prospect of fresh venison for dinner was tantalizing, and Terence followed the trail. Skirting a shallow, brackish pond, green with scum, Terence heard a voice. Silently, he sank to the ground and looked about, but though the voice continued, he could not see its source. At last, having looked all around and seen nothing, Terence glanced at the pond itself and caught his breath.

Through the murky water, Terence could dimly make out an image. Two figures stood in a black and blasted forest. One was a knight, with his visor down, and the other was the most beautiful woman Terence had ever seen. The knight did not move, but the woman was carefully laying out thin twigs in an intricate pattern on the rocky dirt, chanting something in a strange language. As Terence watched, the woman turned toward him, and their eyes met. Terence saw her eyes widen, then grow hard, "Who are you?" she shrieked through the water.

Leaping to his feet, Terence scrambled backwards, throwing himself over a fallen tree, where he almost stepped on a little green figure lying on the path, stretched out comfortably with his hands behind his head.

"Oy! Watch your step, oaf!" the little man shouted. Terence stumbled away from the figure and sat with a heavy crash in the brush. It was the same little sprite who had led Terence to Gawain and had helped him find the Five Kings. The elf grinned and said, "Well, aren't you going to say anything?"

"I wish you'd stop *doing* that to me!" Terence gasped finally.

The little man laughed. He offered Terence his hand and, warily, Terence took it. It was reassuringly warm and solid. Terence had never touched a faery before. Dusting Terence off, the little man said with a chuckle, "If I didn't know better, I'd say you weren't happy to see me. It wounds me, Terence, truly it does. I've a good mind to take myself off."

"Well, I'm not stopping you," Terence muttered. He looked back over the fallen tree at the pond, but the dark water was still.

The sprite grinned again. "I suppose you're wondering why I'm here." Terence didn't reply, still watching the pond. "I thought it was time we were introduced."

"You already seem to know my name," Terence pointed out.

"Yes, but that's all," he said. "I'm a messenger, and I only know what I'm told. As for me, you may call me Robin."

"Pleased to meet you, Robin," Terence said, bowing. "And thank you for your help with the

Five Kings. My master won great glory that day."

"Ah, your master. That reminds me. I've a message for him from the Seelie Court."

"The what?"

"The Seelie Court. Don't ask so many questions. You're to tell him his quest isn't finished yet. Oh no, it's barely begun. Tell him to take the advice of the next relative of his that he meets."

"What relative?"

"You can't expect me to tell you everything, can you?" Robin grinned. "I will say this. You need to get back to your camp now. Things are about to start happening there."

"What things?" Terence asked, but Robin put a finger on his lips and shook his head. "Well, hurry along, lad."

Terence did not move. "One more thing. Who was that woman in the pond?"

Robin's smile slowly faded. "That pond?" he asked. He vaulted lightly over the tree and looked. "I see no woman."

"Oh, don't be stupid," Terence snapped. "You must have heard her scream at me."

"No, Terence. I heard nothing. Tell me about this woman. What was she like?"

"A beautiful woman, with a silent knight beside her." Terence hesitated, peering closely at the faery. "Look here, Robin, are you having me on? Is this another of your tricks?"

"Nay, lad. What was the woman doing?"

"Laying sticks in a design on the ground. And singing something, but I couldn't understand. Do you know what she was doing?"

Robin looked grim. "No, I don't. I told you, I'm only a messenger. But I know others who will understand. I will tell them at once." He looked at Terence, wonder in his eyes. "And I saw and heard nothing. I wish I knew just who you are, my Terence."

Terence nodded. "And if you find out, I wish you'd tell me."

Twenty minutes later, Terence stepped out of the woods into the clearing. Gawain and Tor were leaning against a tree talking while their horses grazed nearby. Plogrun sat by the stream polishing armour. Behind them, half in the shadows and obviously unseen by any of the three, a knight in full armour sat on a dappled gray stallion, watching them. Terence's heart jumped, but it was not the same knight he had seen in the pond.

"Milord?" Terence said. Gawain looked up, and Terence pointed at the strange knight.

Gawain looked, then muttered, "Quiet beggar,

isn't he?" Shifting his sword forward, Gawain strode down the meadow toward the knight. About twenty yards from the knight, he called out, "Welcome, stranger. Come and join our camp for the night, if it please you."

The knight did not move; the only motion was the flutter of a thin yellow streamer tied to the knight's lance. Gawain waited a second, then said, "Or if it does not please you to stay here the night, you are welcome to dine with us." Again, the knight remained motionless. "Or is there some other way we can help you?" Gawain asked doggedly.

This time the knight moved. He lowered his lance and pointed it at Gawain's chest. Gawain shifted his weight so that his sword hilt was even more accessible, but he did not touch it.

"Do you want to fight?" Gawain asked.

The stranger did not move. The lance was still pointed at Gawain's chest.

"Look here, do you think you could nod or shake your head or something to let me know if I'm on the right path? I'm in the dark here. Do you want to fight?" Gawain repeated.

The knight nodded.

"Well, that's something, anyway," Gawain grunted. "I suppose it would be a waste of time to ask you why you want to fight a complete stranger."

The knight nodded again.

"If we refuse to fight you, will you go away?"

The knight shook his head.

"All right, then. I'll fight you, if you like," Gawain said disgustedly. He turned, but before he could complete his turn, Tor called to him.

"Never mind, Gawain. I've a mind to see what noise I can make with this silent knight." Tor hoisted himself into his saddle, and Plogrun handed him the one lance that had a point. Gawain started to speak, then shrugged and walked back to where Terence and Plogrun stood. Tor took a position opposite the strange knight, the two raised their lances in salute, and then they galloped at each other. They came together with a deafening crash. Tor's lance flipped in the air, his horse reared, and Tor himself all but flew backwards out of his saddle, landing a clear five yards back. The strange knight quieted his stallion with a pat and then waited patiently for Tor to stand. Stiffly, Tor struggled to his feet and drew his sword, but the knight shook his head. Turning slightly, he pointed his lance at Gawain.

"So what's wrong with swords, then?" Tor demanded angrily.

The strange knight trotted back to his original

position at the far end of the meadow. Lips pursed, Gawain watched him go. "Plogrun, old fellow," he said, "who would you say was the better jouster? Him or me?"

"I was just wondering myself, sir," Plogrun said deliberately.

"What I thought, too," Gawain said. He whistled for Guingalet and climbed into the saddle.

"Fetch your master a lance, Terence!" Plogrun commanded briskly. "That one." He pointed at the lance that Tor had used, still in the meadow. Terence ran to retrieve it, while Tor and Plogrun stood next to Guingalet.

"He hits hard, Gawain," Tor said.

Gawain nodded and trotted over to the position that Tor had taken. Both knights paused for a second; both saluted with their lances; both charged, leaning forward in their saddles, holding their lances steady against the jolting of their horses. They hit each other at the same instant, and both lances exploded into a thousand splinters. Both horses reared and whinnied, and both knights landed on their backs with a thump.

Gawain raised himself, shook his head dazedly, then climbed to his feet, his sword drawn. The other knight sat up, feeling himself tenderly, but he made no effort to rise further. He cleared his throat. Gawain stepped toward him, but he held up his hand.

"Put away your sword. I have no desire to fight you. Or your friend," the knight said. His voice was dry and raspy, and he cleared his throat again.

"Well then, why the devil did you?" Gawain demanded.

"Did I hear your friend call you Gawain?" the knight asked, ignoring Gawain's question.

"He may have. It is my name."

The knight climbed shakily to his feet. "King Arthur's nephew?" Gawain nodded. "Sir Gawain, it is a pleasure to meet you. Pleasure!" He laughed suddenly. "Much, much more than a pleasure. How strange that I, who have longed for words for so long, should recover them only to find them so inadequate!"

Tor walked toward the two, his hand never far from his sword. Gawain nodded toward him. "This is Sir Tor, also of King Arthur's court."

The knight held out his hand. "A pleasure, Sir Tor," he said.

Tor muttered, "More for you than for me," but he took the offered hand.

"I am Sir Marhault of Cornwall. I do apologize for upsetting you, Sir Tor. I'm afraid I owe you an explanation."

"Do you have a tale to tell?" Gawain asked.

"I do. A very short tale, but one that has seemed long to me."

"You shall tell us after dinner," Gawain pronounced. "That is, if you'll stay."

Sir Marhault unlaced his helm and took it off, revealing an open, friendly face. He seemed to be about thirty or thirty-five. "I'd be delighted," he said.

That evening, as the summer daylight finally began to fade, the three knights and two squires sat around a dying fire, comfortably full, and Sir Marhault told his story.

"As I told you," he began, "I am from Cornwall, where Mark is king, Isoult is queen, and I was the flower of knighthood. From my earliest years, I have had stronger sinews and greater agility than my peers, and by dint of much practice and diligent study achieved a great proficiency in the knightly arts. Ere I had truly reached manhood, I had unhorsed the most highly acclaimed knights of Cornwall, including King Mark himself, and I was given great worship by knights and ladies alike. It is not mysterious then, that I should have grown vain, and as the years passed and I conquered ever more young knights, my vanity grew exceeding great.

"Then, just over a year ago, I met a fair lady who much beguiled my jaded eyes; yet would she not disclose her name to me. When I asked her for her reason, she would say merely that she would disclose her name only to the greatest knight of the land. I laughed and boasted to her that such was I, and then said that no knight ever had or ever would defeat me. However, this lady was in sooth an enchantress, acquainted with the future. She told me that someday I should be defeated by one who would claim much greater fame than ever I had earned, and further, she cast a spell over me, saying that until I had tasted defeat myself, I should be unable to boast, yea even to speak again.

"Since that time I have been a silent wanderer, seeking knights with whom to joust, hoping finally to meet one who would match me. Until I met you, though, Sir Gawain, I found none. And now, having been released from the spell, I know that the greatest victory is not won with one's strength but is won over one's own weakness."

Gawain, Tor, and Sir Marhault stayed up late that night, talking over their battles and what Sir Marhault called the knightly arts. Finally, the party broke up, and each crawled thankfully under his blankets. Terence stretched out in his bedding, not far from Gawain's, and waited until everyone's breathing sounded even and quiet. Then, hesitantly, he reached out and touched Gawain on his shoulder.

From the slight jerk of Gawain's body, Terence knew that Gawain had been asleep, so he hurriedly whispered, "Milord?"

"What is it, Terence?" Gawain whispered in reply.

Now that he had managed to get Gawain alone, Terence was not sure how to begin. Somehow, he had felt that his message from Robin was for Gawain's ears alone. He licked his lips uncertainly.

"Terence?" Gawain whispered again. "Is something wrong?"

"No, milord. I . . . I have a message for you."

"What sort of message?" Gawain's whisper had grown softer, but Terence could not mistake the sharpening interest in his tone.

"Milord, have you ever heard of something called 'the Seelie Court'?" Terence asked finally.

"What do you know of the Seelie Court, boy?"

"Nothing, milord. What is it?" Terence pulled himself a few inches closer.

For a moment Gawain said nothing, then he whispered, "The land of the faeries is divided into two, Terence: the Seelie and the Unseelie Courts. The Seelie Court is the court of the benevolent faeries – like the Pechs, the building folk of Scotland, and the Dheena Shee peoples, even the little brownies and so forth. They aren't always friendly, but they aren't by nature evil. The Unseelie Court is made up of hags and ghouls, trolls, goblins, and the like, who all live only to do evil to men." Gawain paused briefly. "Now you tell me where you heard about the Seelie Court."

"I met a . . . a messenger from the Seelie Court today. In the forest."

"You're sure this messenger was from the Seelie Court?"

"He . . . he said he was," Terence faltered.

"So do they all, lad."

"Oh," Terence said.

"Never mind, Terence. What did he say?" Gawain asked softly.

"He said . . . he said that this quest wasn't over yet, and that you're to do whatever the first relative you meet tells you to do."

"What relative?"

"He wouldn't say, milord."

"Is that all?"

Terence hesitated, but decided suddenly that he should tell no one, not even Gawain, about the figures in the water. "Yes, milord."

Again, Gawain was silent for a long time. Finally

he said, "You did right waiting until now to tell me, Terence. Now, let's go to sleep. Tomorrow begins to sound promising." In a few seconds, Gawain whispered faintly, "I knew you were of faery stock. They'd never speak to you like that if you were not." He chuckled faintly. "Good night, little one."

The next morning the three knights sparred with swords in the meadow, and the two squires busied themselves around the camp. Terence had just stepped toward the forest to gather a few more armloads of firewood when he saw the serpent.

It was a thick serpent with an evil-looking triangular head. A faint trail of smoke rose from its flaring nostrils, and a ridge of tiny spikes showed along its back. Terence knew that he was looking at a dragon. It wound sinuously around a slim beech at the edge of the forest, arching its back luxuriously. Terence froze, then slowly backed away. When he neared the camp, he whispered hoarsely, "Plogrun!"

Something in his voice must have alerted Plogrun, and in a second he was at Terence's side. "Glory and saints help us," he whispered. "That's the real thing, it is."

The beast coiled and writhed from its tail to its

head, then hissed loudly and furiously. Both squires jumped. As one, they turned and ran toward the knights. Terence arrived first, gasping, "Milord! Milord!"

"What is it, lad?"

Terence pointed at the serpent, still winding up and down the beech tree. The knights stared at it in silence, then, holding their swords ready, paced toward it. Terence gulped and followed. Plogrun fell in beside him, panting and muttering, "To save a lady, maybe, but why fight a thing like that if you don't have to, that's what I don't know. Live and let live, I say."

They drew near the beast and stopped, each knight measuring it with his eyes. "It's a foul-looking monster indeed," Sir Marhault said.

"Ah," hissed the serpent, "but the foulest of all are sometimes the best, Sir Marhault."

They all jumped, and the creature laughed.

"Have you ever heard of a talking dragon?" Tor asked.

"Nay, Sir Tor. Never," Sir Marhault replied. Gawain only frowned.

"Sure you have never known love until you have loved something foul," the serpent continued. "Which of you fine knights shall have me to wed?" The serpent slithered ecstatically around the slim beech, making low hissing noises and sending out fine steamy mists from its nostrils and parted lips.

"You always were a twisted wench, Morgan," Gawain said suddenly. He grinned and added, "But if you've taken to wooing men in that shape, your age must be telling on you. Bags under the eyes, is it?"

The beast's eyes flashed at him, and in an annoyed voice that showed no trace of serpentine hissing snapped, "I'm only a year older than you, Nephew, and you know it."

"But women show their age so much earlier, don't you think?" Gawain responded sweetly.

The serpent hissed, but after a second it laughed and in the same voice responded, "I'm still enough of a beauty to make pompous knights babble of their victories to impress me." Slowly the serpent began to change: its long tail separated and became two very shapely legs, then an equally shapely woman's body began to appear. Finally, just before her body revealed itself completely, the coils of snakeskin around her neck fell with silky softness over her, and a beautiful fair-haired woman stood before them. Only the faint sheen of her dress reminded them of the serpent that had been there a moment before.

Terence swallowed hard. The woman before him

had hair of a different colour and in some inexplicable way looked younger, but otherwise was almost identical to the woman he had seen in the pond.

Gawain continued pleasantly, "Trollop. Tor, Sir Marhault, this is my old auntie, Morgan Le Fay."

"Wretch," Morgan hissed.

"We have met," Sir Marhault said stiffly. The woman laughed, and Gawain looked at Sir Marhault with understanding dawning in his face.

"Of course, I should have guessed. Who but my dear auntie would have put you through so much pain? You really are a witch, you know, Morgan."

"I prefer sorceress, little Nephew," she smiled. "And which of you two knights had the honour of breaking my spell and humbling this coxcomb?"

"I did, vixen," Gawain said.

"You? Tsk tsk, will wonders never cease? And just yesterday you were a grubby little brat." She smiled and added, "But we women mature so much sooner, don't you think?"

Gawain's eyes twinkled, and he bowed. "Will you lunch with us today, Auntie?"

"No, no, Marhault would never permit it. Actually, Nevvy, I'm here to help you. I have a bit of advice." Terence stiffened, and Gawain shot him a quick glance.

"Indeed?" Gawain asked pleasantly. "But I should have guessed. You've always been so thoughtful. Less of it, dear! What are you really up to?"

"It is true that I've never shown much interest in you, Gawain – and who shall blame me? Your knightly ideals nauseate me. But you're not the worst of my relations, after all. So, I've put myself out for you today. You are to travel due east. Immediately. That's all." A second later, she had disappeared. The knights looked at each other for a long moment. Then Sir Marhault spoke, "Your aunt, you say."

"My mother's youngest sister." Gawain turned back toward camp. "Well, here's where we part."

"You don't mean that you're going to do what she said?" Sir Marhault demanded, loathing in his voice.

"What would you have me do? If I didn't, I'd spend the rest of my life wondering what would have happened."

Tor smiled. "Must you go it alone, Gawain? I'm rather at loose ends at the moment. Mind if I join you?"

"And I?" Sir Marhault said promptly. "Whatever devilment your aunt is up to, you may be glad of the extra sword."

Gawain nodded. "Come along, if you like."

And so, within the hour they were off. Again they followed the narrow forest track that had led them to the meadow. Gawain and Terence led the way, slowly pulling ahead of the others.

"It looks as though your messenger was serious, Terence," Gawain said quietly.

"Yes, milord," Terence replied.

"But it doesn't tell us whether he meant us good or evil. Morgan is just as likely to have dealings with the Unseelie Court as the Seelie. You can never tell with her. I've seen her turn a man to dust for rudeness, but I've also seen her gathering wildflowers with a child."

And then the dark path brightened, and the little cavalcade burst out of the forest into a bright, sunlit clearing. In the centre of the clearing was an ancient stone well with wild carving all over it. Behind the well, three white mares were saddled, and on a bench nearby sat three ladies in flowing silken robes. One was an ancient lady with a fine network of wrinkles on her neck and face, but with a bright, piercing gleam in her eyes. The second was a lady of about thirty-five or forty, with a look of experience but with a quiet beauty that had been untouched by time. The last lady was no more than nineteen years old and was strikingly beautiful.

7

ALISOUN THE BLOODTHIRSTY

Terence rode behind Gawain and the young beauty, listening to her inexhaustible flow of inconsequential conversation. The three had been riding for over two hours, and not once in that time had the lady – Lady Alisoun, her name was – stopped talking. She chattered about the other knights she had ridden with, their weapons, their admiration of her beauty, and especially about their fights. Terence, who had developed a deep dislike for Lady Alisoun, heartily wished that things had happened differently at the well.

When the three knights had ridden up to the well, the three ladies had smiled and welcomed them graciously. The lady of about thirty-five years swept a low, elegant curtsey and said, "We welcome three questing knights. Come and water your horses."

Sir Marhault bowed. "We greet you, fair ladies, and thank you." The ladies waited in silence while the travellers dipped water from the well. Then Sir Marhault turned back to the lady who had spoken and said, "If we may ask, how came you to know that we are on quest?"

The lady smiled and answered, "No knight ever finds this well save he is on quest. When you are refreshed, each of you will choose one of us to ride with you, and we shall take you to find adventures. At an arranged time, we shall return here to tell our tales. We are the Three Questing Ladies."

Sir Marhault looked startled. "This is what you wish, my lady?" he asked. She nodded and smiled again. He looked at Gawain and Tor. "What say you, friends?"

"I say the same thing I said when Morgan sent me this way: we have to try it, or we'll wonder the rest of our lives what would have happened," Gawain said.

Tor and Sir Marhault nodded. Terence glanced at Plogrun and was surprised to see the dwarf's face rigid with impotent fury. The dwarf's eyes were fixed on the eldest of the ladies.

"Shall we say, then, that we return in three

months' time?" asked the lady who seemed to speak for them all. The knights looked at each other and nodded. "Very well," she continued. "Now you shall choose. Who is first?"

For a moment, none of the knights spoke. Then Sir Marhault said, "Sir Tor, you choose."

"Very well," Tor said. He looked thoughtfully at the three then said, "I am the youngest and least experienced of us, and so I choose the most experienced of you." He looked at the ancient lady. "Should you like to accompany me, madam?"

A glow of triumph in her eyes, the old lady rose and laughed. "I knew it! I willed you to choose me!"

"Glory and saints preserve us!" Plogrun interjected with loathing. "Of all the women in the world, you choose this one!"

"What—?" Tor began, but the woman cut him off.

"And it's a good thing he did, too," she retorted. "I'll have my hands full trying to unlearn him whatever foolishness you've been drilling into his head."

Plogrun turned a deep red and said, "Sir, if you please, perhaps you'd like to choose someone else."

A muscle quivered at the edge of Tor's mouth, and he said, "Are you acquainted with the lady

113

already?"

"Lady Lyne here – if you can call her a lady, and if you think it's ladylike to spend more time with swords and lances than with sewing and music, then I don't know where your wits have gone – as I say, this *lady* and I met some years ago."

Tor raised his eyebrows and started to speak, but again the lady spoke before he could say anything. "Not so long ago that I don't remember how your precious Sir Linas ended up on his back in the dirt. I'll swear you taught him all you knew, too."

"Humph! As if anyone could teach that dolt. If I *had* taught him, he would have had your Sir Monocus down in a trice!"

"Plogrun," Tor said firmly, "I will have no squire serve me who is uncivil to a lady."

Plogrun clamped his mouth shut, still seething. The lady looked triumphantly at the dwarf, then said to Tor, "Quite right, Sir Tor. I see no need for a squire at all, in fact."

"Even," Tor continued, still looking at Plogrun, "when the lady is herself uncivil." Lady Lyne reddened, and Plogrun's eyes gleamed. Tor turned back to the lady. "Which direction, madam?" he asked politely.

Without speaking, the lady pointed south and lightly mounted her horse. Tor gave Gawain one expressive look, rolled his eyes, and they were off.

As soon as they had disappeared into the forest, the lady who did the speaking said, "Who shall be next?"

"Choose, Marhault," Gawain said.

"I thank you, Gawain," Sir Marhault said. He looked at the lady of middle years and smiled courteously at her. "If it should be agreeable to you, I feel I would delight in your company, my lady," he said.

"It is agreeable," she said, returning his smile. Gracefully, she stood and walked to her horse. Sir Marhault helped her into her saddle. She pointed north, and in a moment they were gone.

"And so, it seems, the most beautiful of all is left for me," Gawain said, giving the youngest lady the smile that he had used so effectively among the ladies of Camelot. "I could not have asked for better fortune." Gawain bowed gallantly.

She dimpled at him, pleased, and said, "My name is Alisoun, and I'm very glad that you chose me, because you were the one that sounded the most gallant of all of them when you said that you couldn't pass by an adventure. That's what a knight really ought to be like, don't you think? Never passing up any chance to fight to the death and kill recreant knights and dragons and giants

115

and die a glorious death in the end. It's a hard and brutal life, don't you think? I do, but how anyone could want any other sort of life than that I simply cannot imagine, can you? Well, I can tell you, I've met so many cowardly knights, running away from fights for simply the smarmiest reasons that you wouldn't credit it, not if I told you. Oh no, don't bother helping me into the saddle. I'm not so puny as all that. In fact, one knight that I rode with even let me keep his spare sword. He said I was to fall on it if ever he was killed, but of course I didn't listen to him, because simply all of my knights get killed. It's a very lowering thought, I can tell you. But I kept the sword all the same, not to fall on, of course, but to use if I ever got stuck in a fight. Do you think it's unladylike to know how to fight with a sword? I don't, and I feel sure that Lady Lyne doesn't, though she never says anything about it in front of me. You know, I sometimes have the idea that she talks a great deal more when she's with other people than she does when she's with me."

"Imagine!" Gawain said.

And that, Terence thought, was the last time that Gawain had spoken. For two hours now Lady Alisoun had described bloody jousts and bloodier sword fights that she had seen and the various knights she had ridden with, all of whom seemed to have earned great glory before being cut off in the prime of their lives by some recreant knight or another. Lady Alisoun talked a lot about recreant knights, by which she apparently meant any knight with whom she did not herself ride, but she held no grudges against them, and described their prowess in killing her escorts in the same glowing terms which she used to describe her own knights' deeds.

"And then," Lady Alisoun was saying, "after cutting Sir Nimilake's legs off at the knees, Sir Winchell laid one of them at my feet, saying that it was my own inspiration which inspired him to win so awful a fight in such a sanguine way, which really was not very pleasant because it was still bleeding, of course, but which was really very touching, all things considered. I do think Sir Winchell may have been the greatest knight who's ever served me, because he had such a flair for the dramatic, don't you think so? At least he did until Sir Abelleus killed him with a mace. I don't think people ought to be allowed to use maces in combat, because, for one thing, they're really not much different from clubs, which seems so unrefined, and if there's anything I can't stand, it's something that's unrefined."

"Did you say Sir Abelleus?" Gawain interrupted.

"That's right. Oh, he's a terrible fighter, he is, a regular Heckler of Troy. He's as strong as an ox. I hope we meet him again, so you can kill him for me."

"I don't think I'll be able to," Gawain commented.

That silenced Lady Alisoun, though only for a second, while she gaped at Gawain. "Well, I don't mean he's *that* fierce," she said finally.

Gawain grinned at her and said, "I mean Abelleus is already dead."

Lady Alisoun clapped her hands joyfully and said, "Wonderful! Oh, wonderful! Did you kill him?"

"I'm afraid not, but I was there when it happened, and I promise you that he bled freely. Sir Tor, the young knight I was with earlier, did the actual killing."

"Oh." She looked regretfully over her shoulder. "Well, how did it happen?"

"He cut off his head," Gawain said.

"Perfect! Just what Abelleus did to Sir Winchell! What did he do with the head? Abelleus stepped on Sir Winchell's head."

Gawain looked solemn. "Well, there was a lady there at the time who had shown herself to be bloodthirsty beyond what is fitting in a lady – or in fact in anyone – so Sir Tor tied Abelleus's head around her neck."

"Oh," Lady Alisoun said.

"Fitting, don't you think?" Gawain asked blandly.

"Oh yes," she agreed after a second. "I can't stand women who are unladylike, can you?"

"I don't really know what is ladylike and what is not, but I certainly couldn't stand this lady."

Terence chuckled, and Lady Alisoun glanced sharply back at him. She looked back at Gawain. "Have you ever cut off someone's head?"

Gawain frowned for a second, then said, "If I have, would you consider it a great deed?"

"Oh yes," she said immediately.

"Then it wouldn't be very knightly of me to boast, would it? A knight should be modest."

"Oh, but you don't have to be modest in front of me. I'm your lady, after all."

"On the contrary," Gawain said firmly. "A knight should be especially modest in front of a lady."

"Oh," Lady Alisoun said, frowning. "But if you don't tell anyone about your great deeds, people might think you haven't done any at all."

Gawain shook his head very slightly. "But that's the whole point, don't you think?"

Lady Alisoun looked confused, but she pressed on. "No. To do great deeds and then keep them secret sounds absolutely daftheaded to me. I perfectly understand that a knight mustn't *seem* boastful, but you could tell me about your great deeds, and then I could tell others." Gawain only shook his head. "Well I never!" Lady Alisoun said, exasperated. "Don't you *want* people to know your triumphs?"

"Oh yes," Gawain said. "Very much. In fact, that's why I keep them secret: because I suspect I want them known rather too much."

"I don't understand you at all!" Lady Alisoun said, and for once Terence sympathized with her.

"I can't blame you for that," Gawain said agreeably. He touched Guingalet with his heel and trotted ahead of Lady Alisoun.

Soon the forest thinned and the travellers began to come upon settled lands: farms, grazing lands, and on a distant rise what looked like a castle. Gawain slowed then stopped, saying, "Do you hear something, Terence?"

Terence listened to the wind. "Horses, milord. Quite a few of them."

"Let's go see. Maybe we can cut off someone's limbs for Lady Alisoun," Gawain said. They topped a rise and saw a field full of knights in armour. On one side of the field were ten knights in a silent row. On the other side, one knight sat his horse alone. While they watched, the first of the row of knights lowered his lance and charged the lone knight. The lone knight unhorsed his attacker easily and trotted back to his side of the field. Then the second knight attacked, and the lone knight knocked him head over ears into the dirt. The third knight met the same fate. Terence glanced at Gawain, who was watching the proceedings with a smile.

"Well?" Lady Alisoun said witheringly. Gawain looked at her in polite surprise.

"Well what?" Gawain asked.

"Aren't you going to do anything?"

Gawain frowned. "What would you like me to do, my lady?"

"Help that poor knight who is fighting alone of course!"

"Does he appear to you to need help?" The fourth and fifth knights went down before the lone knight's lance.

"Don't you think ten against one is unchivalrous?" Lady Alisoun demanded.

"I do. But this is ten times one against one. When they all attack him at once I'll go help."

"You know what I think? I think you're afraid!"

Gawain gave her a brief glance that indicated no interest whatsoever, and she lapsed into a furious silence.

The three of them watched until the last of the ten knights had been unhorsed. "Here now, what's this?" Gawain said.

The lone knight had dismounted and was walking toward the cluster of defeated knights, holding his hands out before him. Immediately, the ten knights bound his hands securely and began slapping him and spitting on his armour. The lone knight made no move to defend himself. While Gawain and his party watched, one of the ten knights caught the lone knight's horse. Shouting triumphantly, the ten knights looped ropes around the lone knight, tying him to the underside of his horse, his face looking up between his horse's hind legs.

"What is he doing, milord?" Terence gasped.

"I haven't a clue, Terence."

"Now will you go help him?" Lady Alisoun demanded.

"I can do many things," Gawain commented, "but I can't help someone who doesn't want help. If he didn't want to look up his horse's nether eye, he could have just ridden away."

"You think he wanted to end up like that?" Lady

Alisoun was scornful.

"Seems so, doesn't it?"

"That's ridiculous!"

"Can't argue with that," Gawain replied. They watched while the ten defeated knights mounted and rode off, leading their humiliated captive. When they were out of sight, Gawain said, "Let's move on."

Lady Alisoun looked at Gawain with such contempt on her face that Terence itched to shake her and tell her all about Gawain's battles with Ablamor and Alardin and Hautubris, but if Gawain chose to let her think he was afraid, then Terence would too. Ten minutes later, two knights met them on the path. One was of medium build and wore a jaunty feather in his helm, and the other was considerably larger and wore his visor down.

"Hello," the knight with the feather called. "Come far?"

"Good day," Gawain answered. "Not too far, just from the forest."

"Off questing, eh?" The knight grinned. He had a fair, pleasant face, and a few strands of sandy hair framed his face within his open helm.

"Ay. You?" Gawain responded.

"No, not questing exactly, but so long as I've put

this bleeding armour on, I wouldn't mind seeing a bit of action. I don't suppose you'd like to take a few passes with me in joust, would you?"

To Terence's surprise, Gawain agreed immediately. The jousting posts were decided upon in a nearby pasture, and the two rode off, leaving Terence, Lady Alisoun and the other knight alone to watch. The first pass ended with no one the worse. Gawain had wheeled Guingalet to the left just before the lances came together, making the fair knight's lance miss him by several feet, while Gawain tapped him on the back with the point of his lance as he went by. The fair knight laughed and shouted something over his shoulder. Lady Alisoun grunted, "Just the sort of cowardly motion I'd expect from him." Terence flushed angrily.

On the second pass, Gawain unhorsed the fair knight neatly, then dismounted and suggested swords for a while. The two knights began sparring with their swords, circling each other slowly, choosing their hits carefully. The fair knight was not a bad swordsman, but even to Terence's inexperienced eye it seemed that Gawain was not trying very hard.

For the first time, the knight with the hidden face spoke, to Lady Alisoun. "Have you some reason, fair lady, to doubt your knight's courage?"

Lady Alisoun laughed scornfully. "Not half an hour ago we saw one knight pitted against ten, and this yellow dog refused to help him. Even when the ten knights captured their valiant foe in the most humiliating way, he would do nothing!"

Terence gasped. "It wasn't like that at all!" he declared hotly.

The knight leaned menacingly over his saddle, his hand on his sword hilt, and said, "Do not contradict a lady, boy, else you shall taste my blade." Terence stared at him, shocked. No knight of Arthur's court would ever have threatened a squire.

"See? He doesn't even teach his squire well," Lady Alisoun declared, pink with pleasure.

The knight turned back to her. "It is indeed a pity that so entrancing a lady should be bound to so wanting a knight."

"Oh, I'm not *bound* to him, exactly," she said, her eyes downcast.

"No? Ah, but perhaps it is best that you should have such a knight to follow. He will do his best to avoid danger, and thus you shall be spared the sight of pain and suffering."

"I don't mind pain and suffering," she said earnestly.

"Do you not? But then you have not seen the sort of bloody battles which I fight every day. I promise you, it is no sight for a lady."

"Really?" Lady Alisoun's eyes shone. "Very bloody?"

"Horribly," he replied promptly.

"I wish I could see them," she responded rapturously.

"Why, you can, if you choose to ride away with me, now, my lady," the knight said. "Since you have plighted no troth to this knight, of course."

Lady Alisoun did not hesitate, "Yes, let's!"

Terence could not believe it. Before he could decide whether to say anything, they were gone. He turned back toward the sparring knights, wondering if Gawain would be angry with him for letting her go.

About half an hour later, panting and wheezing with exertion, the fair knight held up his hand and said, "Enough! You're just playing with me, aren't you?"

Gawain raised his visor and grinned. "Well, yes. A bit."

"It's too hot to continue. What do you say to a tankard of the best home-brewed ale in the country? There's an inn just over the way where they take real pride in such things."

"Sounds wonderful." Gawain smiled. "I'm Sir Gawain, from Camelot."

"Camelot? Really? Do you mean I fought a knight of the Round Table?"

"You did."

"Well, won't father be tickled! I'm Sir Carados. My father's the Earl hereabouts, and— I say, where's your lady? And that other knight?"

"Don't you know that other knight?" Gawain asked.

"No, we'd just met when we came up to you. Where are they?"

"They left some time ago," Gawain replied, unperturbed. He smiled at Terence and said, "My only fear was that you would interfere, lad, and convince her to stay. You don't mind losing her, do you, Terence?"

Terence sighed happily.

An hour later, seated around a table with three tankards of smooth, warm beer in front of them, Gawain turned to his new companion and asked, "Say, Carados, as the Earl's son, you must know most of the people in the area."

"All of them, I expect," Sir Carados said, wiping froth from his lips.

"Today we saw an interesting sight: one knight

fought ten, defeated them, and then let them tie him up and take him away. Now who—"

"Odd, isn't it? He does it all the time," Sir Carados interrupted.

"Why?"

"Sad, really. Those knights belong to the lady he loves, the Lady Ettard. You probably saw her castle on your way in, on that hill to the east. He lets them take him captive, because that's the only way he can see her."

Gawain blinked. "I see," he said. "Then I could find him at Lady Ettard's castle tomorrow?"

"I doubt it. She usually throws him out after a night in her dungeons."

"Where might I find him, then?"

"Dalinbrook Castle, hard by the forest, not two hours from here," Sir Carados said. "His name's Sir Pelleas."

8

PELLEAS THE STUPID

At nine o'clock the next morning, after a pleasant evening spent with Sir Carados's family, Gawain and Terence arrived at Sir Pelleas's Dalinbrook Castle. The gate was open, and a few servants stood around, listlessly sweeping the path.

"Seems he's not home yet," Gawain said.

They waited outside the gate for about twenty minutes before Sir Pelleas arrived, carrying his helm on his saddle. His armour was dusty and stained, and his face drawn and weary. When he saw Gawain and Terence, though, he stopped abruptly, looked almost pleased, replaced his helm, and readied his lance.

"Sir Pelleas!" Gawain called.

"Make ready for battle, recreant knight!" Sir Pelleas shouted back.

"I'm not a recreant knight, and I won't make ready for battle!" Gawain replied promptly.

"I beg your pardon?" Sir Pelleas raised his visor and looked at Gawain, puzzled.

"And I'm not from Lady Ettard," Gawain added.

"Oh, I see." Sir Pelleas drooped. "Well, what do you want, then?"

"I'm a wandering knight in search of adventures. I would like to hear more about your plight. Perhaps I can help."

Sir Pelleas trotted closer, his face downcast. "I thank you for your offer, O knight, but there is no help for one such as I. My life is doomed to despair and disappointment."

"Oh, I daresay it's not so bad as all that," Gawain said bracingly. "Perhaps you could tell me about it inside." He gestured toward the open gate. "After you've cleaned up, of course," he added.

Sir Pelleas sighed deeply, then said, "Very well. To recount my woes can only be painful to me, but I shall grant your wishes, I, whose own wishes are so far from being granted."

An hour later, Sir Pelleas joined Gawain and Terence in a sombre, rather chilly room. "Forgive me for taking so long, O knight. Lady Ettard's dungeons have a great many insects."

Sir Pelleas was a strong-looking, exceptionally handsome knight, with a carefully trimmed chestnut beard covering a firm chin. He wore a richly woven maroon blouse, trimmed all over with gold lace, and burnished black stockings. If he was a bit sober in appearance, he was at least elegant. "I am Sir Gawain, of the Fellowship of the Round Table," Gawain said. "I am sworn to help those in distress, and so I offer you whatever services are in my power."

"I thank you," Sir Pelleas said. "But nothing is in your power."

"Suppose you tell me your . . . your woes," Gawain invited.

Sir Pelleas sighed and signed for Gawain to be seated. Terence stood beside his chair while Sir Pelleas paced.

"I love the most beautiful woman in the world," he began, his eyes fixed dreamily on the rafters. "She is the most perfect example of ladyhood to be found. In no matter is she lacking. Her nose is a vessel of beauty, straight and white, which no desecrating freckle has ever been permitted to touch. I've written a sonnet to her nose. Would you like to hear it? It goes: *'J'entends de la musique, c'est son museau, son nez—'"*

Gawain choked. Sir Pelleas stopped reciting and

waited patiently. Gawain spoke before he could continue. "In French, of course."

"The language of love," Sir Pelleas sighed.

"But you're not a French-speaker yourself, are you?"

"Well, I'm not really fluent, but—"

"Yes, well, my own French is a touch rusty," Gawain said, "but I don't think you should call your lady's nose a *museau*. It means snout."

"Really? But I thought that the similarity in sound with *musique* was so effective."

"Ah, I daresay I'm mistaken," Gawain said affably. "I think, though, that I have grasped the perfection of your lady's nose. Perhaps we can move on."

"Ah, her eyebrows . . ." Sir Pelleas sighed dreamily. Gawain let out his breath and sank into his chair. After close to half an hour of rapturous description that included eyebrows, eyelashes, eyes, ears, hair, cheeks, neck, waist and a full ten minutes on lips, Sir Pelleas caught his breath with a sob and concluded, "But she'll have none of me!"

Gawain let him sob for a moment, then said, "And . . . what made you fall in love with this paragon?"

Sir Pelleas looked surprised. "Can you doubt it?

132

It was love at first sight!"

"I see. But you *have* spoken to her, haven't you?"

"I am a newcomer to this land. I had never spoken to her before I pledged her my undying love."

"Look, Pelleas, are you sure you're not making a mistake? I don't mean to say that your love isn't deep and profound and all that, but shouldn't you know something more about a woman than her looks?" Gawain paused, frowning, then continued, "I rode into this country yesterday alongside a very beautiful lady who had no more heart than a spider. I've only just managed to get rid of her."

Sir Pelleas leaped to his feet. "What are you implying?" he demanded.

Gawain did not move. Calmly he replied, "Nothing at all. I only wondered if you ought to speak to the Lady Ettard. Have you ever just ridden up and asked to come in?" Gawain asked.

"Oh yes!" Sir Pelleas said. "But to no avail! The foulest of wandering knights may be sure of a welcome from her, but *I* am turned away . . . but I . . . but I . . . but I have an idea!"

Gawain looked amused. "What kind of idea?"

"I shall go to her in disguise! I shall go with you!

In your retinue! She will admit you to her court, and then I shall expose to her my love from within!"

Gawain nodded. "Not bad. You go put on something that looks like a squire might wear it, and we'll go see this lady of yours." Sir Pelleas started to run from the room, but Gawain stopped him. "Say, does Lady Ettard speak French?"

"But of course!"

"Then leave the sonnets here, all right?"

The plan worked perfectly. At the gate to Lady Ettard's castle, Gawain simply called out his name, and the guards opened the gate immediately. No one even looked at Sir Pelleas. A series of calls echoed from guardpost to guardpost – "Open for Sir Dwayne." Gawain chuckled.

A window in the central keep of the castle flew open and there appeared the face of a lovely woman. "Sir Dwayne!" she called out. "I am the Lady Ettard, mistress of this castle. I welcome you!"

Gawain had no chance to answer. Sir Pelleas threw himself from his saddle, and knelt. "My princess!" he called out. "My love, my lambkin! I swear to you eternal fealty. My own life I offer you! My corpse I give to you for a rug, if you so desire! I worship you!"

"Ghastly display," Gawain muttered.

"Pelleas! How did you—? You blister! Get out of my castle! I forbid you to drool on my courtyard, you mutt, you cur, you mongrel! How dare you defile my home with your foul presence? Sir Dwayne, is this your doing?"

Gawain started to reply, but Sir Pelleas broke in again. "My angel, your voice drips sweetness upon my thirsting ears. Speak yet again that I might carry your musical essence with me until I die!"

"I'll drip sweetness on you, you carbuncle!" She called a command to someone inside, then looked back out. "And I hope that you might learn a lesson from it, you less-than-the-stable-sweepings bit of offal! You stench! You *merde!*"

"Ah, she *does* speak French," Gawain murmured.

"My heart! Even curses from your lips fall like blessings on my parched soul. You are the water that revives me!" Sir Pelleas called out.

"Here! Revive on this!" Lady Ettard shouted. She reached inside for something, then at arm's length poured the contents of a large bucket over Sir Pelleas. The mixture seemed to be mostly dirty water, but there were thick clumps of every conceivable colour and texture swirled in. The stream hit Sir Pelleas full in his upturned face and knocked him sprawling into a thick, slimy puddle.

"Kitchen swill!" Terence gasped, wrinkling his nose.

"Not especially fresh either," Gawain agreed. "Let's move upwind, shall we?"

Gawain and Terence edged their horses to where the smell was not so strong. Sir Pelleas climbed to his feet, pulling something from his hair, and called, "I accept this and all other blessings which have known the delight of your presence, fair one!"

Lady Ettard's eyes flashed, and she disappeared inside. Sir Pelleas continued calling out compliments to the window.

"Milord?" Terence asked.

"Yes?"

"This Sir Pelleas, milord? He's . . . he's not very clever, is he?"

Gawain grinned, but did not answer. Lady Ettard reappeared at the window, a triumphant smile on her face. In her arms was a basket filled with eggs. She began throwing them at Pelleas, and Terence noted with respect that she was quite accurate.

"It's a real pleasure to see a lady of gentle birth with such a fine throwing arm," Gawain said solemnly. "Good wrist action, too."

Servants and guards who were downwind from Pelleas began to scurry for cover, and even upwind where Gawain and Terence sat a noxious, sour smell began to grow. Pelleas sniffed bemusedly at himself as Lady Ettard threw her last eggs.

"Now, guards!" Lady Ettard called. "Take him and beat him with boards!"

"Here we go, Terence," Gawain muttered, drawing his sword and winding his reins around a bolt in his saddle. "You get his horse."

Terence galloped to Sir Pelleas's horse. It shied away, but leaning from his saddle he caught the horse's bridle and turned toward the gate. Gawain had Sir Pelleas by the collar, dragging him beside Guingalet at arm's length, and keeping four guards at bay with the other hand. Terence booted his own horse into the middle of the guards, knocking them flying. Another guard ran up, thrusting a spear, and Terence dodged, feeling it pass an inch from his face. He kicked the spearman in the face, and rode past. Gawain barked a syllable to Guingalet, and the mighty horse jumped into a dead run toward the gate, where a line of guards was forming. Guingalet hit the first one with his shoulder, and the line disappeared as guards scattered. Terence followed in Guingalet's wide wake. In a few seconds they were clear of the gate and galloping down the hill into the forest, Sir Pelleas still hanging from Gawain's left hand.

Soon after entering the forest, they came upon a small stream, and Gawain unceremoniously tossed Sir Pelleas into the middle of it. Sir Pelleas gasped and spluttered, then sat up and moaned, "Oh, what am I to do?"

"Clean off," Gawain commanded, looking distastefully at the hand that had touched Sir Pelleas's clothes. "Then we'll eat some lunch and plan our next move."

"How can I eat? Food has no attraction for me!"

"Until you clean up, food will have no attraction for any of us," Gawain snapped. "Now wash!"

Sir Pelleas cleaned himself and his clothes as much as he could while Terence hurriedly put together a meal. When they had eaten, Gawain sat next to Sir Pelleas and said, "Is that how you act every time you're around her?"

"Yes, of course. How could I act differently? Love overpowers every faculty, and I yield myself to its urgings."

"I see. What you need, Pelleas, is an emissary, someone who can represent your case without emptying the butter tub over her."

"Emptying the—"

"Covering her with foolish compliments. Now you wait here, and Terence and I will go see what we can do for you. All right?"

"Do you want to take her a sonnet? I have one that I've been sav—"

"No."

So Gawain and Terence rode back up the hill toward Lady Ettard's castle, leaving the damp and still stained Sir Pelleas in the forest. As they rode, Gawain looked Terence over approvingly and said, "You did well in that bit of rough-and-tumble in the courtyard. Very well."

Terence blushed. "Thank you, milord."

To their surprise, the gate was raised as soon as they approached. Gawain lifted his eyebrows, but led the way back into the courtyard. There, they were met by a thin, dapper gentleman in velvet who bowed slightly to them and asked if he could be of service. Gawain asked to see Lady Ettard, and the dapper gentleman said, "Follow me, please."

They dismounted and followed him through a long hallway to a small inner court. He said, "You may wait here, and my lady will see you if she finds time."

"Why don't you go in and tell her that it's not

convenient for us to wait?" Gawain smiled.

The dapper gentleman looked affronted. In a cold voice, he said, "My lady is engaged in some urgent business."

"Why, so are we," Gawain said. "You run along and tell her, and we'll go with you." He pushed the gentleman through the door and down the hall. A moment later, almost carrying the servant aloft ahead of him, Gawain entered a chamber where Lady Ettard sat at a table with two ladies-in-waiting.

She really was very pretty, Terence thought. It was hard for Terence to associate the delicate figure seated in the stateroom with the screaming woman who had emptied the swill on Sir Pelleas. She leaned forward, peered at Gawain, frowned, and said earnestly, "What are you doing with Brundle, Sir Dwayne?"

Gawain let go of the gentleman, who scurried from the room. "Nothing inappropriate, I assure you," Gawain said politely.

Lady Ettard frowned, as if trying to solve a puzzle, but in a moment her brow lightened, and she said, "Well, never mind. What can I do for you, Sir Dwayne?"

"I come as an ambassador. From Sir Pelleas—"

"That weakling!" Lady Ettard interjected

scornfully.

"It seems to me," Gawain said mildly, "that you are in the position to know that he is hardly a weakling. I myself saw him unhorse ten of your knights in a row."

"And then what did he do? He surrendered to them and let them abuse him! I say he is a weakling."

"Do you not think, madam, that it takes strength of decision to accept abuse without responding in kind?"

"No, I think it takes a great deal of foolishness. I prefer a man who takes what he wants."

"You would prefer to be tyrannized than cherished? Bullied than beloved?" Gawain asked. Terence glanced at him and saw a suspicious light in his eyes.

"'Tyrannized than cherished,'" she repeated, frowning intently. "That's very good. And 'bullied than—' what was that again?" She looked like a schoolgirl committing a difficult sum to memory. "Anyway, I have no admiration for a man who would allow himself to be beaten. Pelleas would be very uncomfortable by now if you had not acted so swiftly."

Gawain hesitated, then said, "I did what any true knight would have done, madam."

"So I saw," Lady Ettard said demurely. Terence caught his breath and looked askance at Gawain, hoping to warn him, but Gawain was smiling that devilishly effective smile of his. Terence closed his eyes and shook his head slowly. "You seem also to dislike being kept waiting, Dwayne," Lady Ettard added, looking shyly at the door through which the discomposed Brundle had scuttled.

"I admit, my lady, that I was perhaps a bit overeager to . . . to see you," Gawain said. "I do hope I haven't inconvenienced your servant."

"Oh no," Lady Ettard said vacuously. "Brundle won't mind. He . . . he is not used to dealing with such men as you."

Gawain smiled even more broadly. "Perhaps," he said after a moment, "I should send my squire away, so that we could talk privately."

"If you like," Lady Ettard smiled faintly.

"He shall run some errands for me," Gawain said. "You'd like that, wouldn't you, Terence?" Terence sighed sadly, but he nodded. Gawain pulled Terence to one side and whispered quickly, "Go get Pelleas. Bring him here at once. Tell him Lady Ettard has changed her mind. Got that?" Terence blinked dazedly, but he nodded. "Good," Gawain said with a chuckle. "It looks as though we'll wind this business up, after all."

Terence found Sir Pelleas gazing abstractedly at the stream by their camp. Mindful of his instructions, Terence said, "Lady Ettard has changed her mind, and you're to go to her at once." Pelleas leaped to his feet, his face shining with delight, and chattered, "Did she say she loved me after all? Will she marry me? What did Sir Gawain say? Did he tell her how much I loved her?"

Fortunately for Terence, who could not think of answers to any of these questions, Sir Pelleas did not wait for a reply. Sir Pelleas leaped onto his horse, his wet pants smacking loudly on the saddle, and together they galloped back up the hill to the castle.

"Where is she?" Sir Pelleas demanded.

"This way, sir." Terence led him down the long hallway, through the entrance court into the stateroom. It was empty except for a lone housemaid cleaning the fireplace. "But— where's Lady Ettard? Excuse me, miss. Where's your mistress?"

"Oh, I don't think I should say," the girl tittered. "Her not being, as you say, receiving visitors."

"Look here, girl," Sir Pelleas demanded. "Lady Ettard is expecting me right now!"

She gaped at him in amazement. "You don't say! I never heard of such goings on! I never!"

"Where *is* she?" Sir Pelleas asked again.

"She's in the garden – right through that door." The girl pointed, her eyes still wide.

Sir Pelleas flung open the door. There, on a stone bench in a fragrant garden, sat Lady Ettard and Gawain. As Sir Pelleas opened the door, Gawain leaned forward and gave Lady Ettard a long kiss on the lips. Terence closed his eyes in anguish.

"What is the meaning of this?" Sir Pelleas roared. Gawain stood quickly, and stared at Sir Pelleas, wide-eyed. Sir Pelleas wore no sword, but one lay on a table near the door, easily to hand, and he grasped it and strode toward the bench. Gawain made no move to defend himself, but instead knelt at Sir Pelleas's feet, abject terror on his face.

"Sir Pelleas! How— oh, please don't kill me!" he cried. Terence stared.

"Traitor! You should be flogged like a lackey!" Sir Pelleas shouted furiously.

"Oh no, please no! I'll do anything! I'll be your squire, your groom, your stable sweep! Only let not your mighty wrath fall on me!" Gawain bowed his head, a picture of fear, but before he lowered his eyes he gave Terence a sharp warning glance.

"Thou coward! I should kill thee now," Sir Pelleas declared grandly, "but I do not wish to sully this blade with thy craven blood!"

"Dwayne!" Lady Ettard said faintly. She was looking from one knight to the other in consternation.

"He is too strong for me, my lady!" Gawain whimpered.

"Pelleas!" she said, her eyes shining. "You . . . you are . . . oh, Pelleas!" She clasped her hands together rapturously. "Pelleas, throw this craven dog out of my castle – and then, and then come back, if you like."

Terence saw Gawain's shoulders shaking with a barely suppressed mirth. He began to grin himself as he finally understood Gawain's plan and saw how it had worked. Sir Pelleas, driven to jealous fury, was at last the sort of man whom Lady Ettard desired.

"Come back to you?" Sir Pelleas snapped contemptuously to Lady Ettard. "I should rather come back to a pit of garbage!" Gawain's head snapped up, and he stared incredulously as Sir Pelleas continued. "You have been false to me once; I shall never allow it to happen again!"

"Pelleas! I was blind! I did not see your strength, your might, your . . . your beauty."

"I am proof to your trickery, the wiles of a faithless woman!" Sir Pelleas laughed. "You would throw yourself at some other wandering knight –

or squire or lackey – in a day! Trollop! Doxy!"

Lady Ettard burst into hysterical sobs, wailing, "Oh Pelleas, my love, my love," between gasps. Gawain stood up, exasperated.

"Pelleas," he whispered urgently, "don't be a—"

"On your knees, villain!" Sir Pelleas commanded, raising his sword threateningly.

"You witless ninny! Will you listen to me?" Gawain whispered fiercely.

"I told thee to kneel!" Sir Pelleas roared.

"Will you be quiet for one minute? Look! She's yours, I tell you!"

"I want none of her, after thy foul lips have touched her," he shouted, even louder. Lady Ettard burst into fresh gusts of tears. Sir Pelleas raised his head proudly, "I shall retire to some holy place and breathe my last, surrendering this vain world forever! Now, for the last time, kneel, thou cur!"

"Oh shut it!" Gawain said crossly. Sir Pelleas made as though to raise his sword, but Gawain plucked it from his hand and tossed it across the garden. "Go and breathe your last or whatever it is you want to do. I wash my hands of you!"

"I shall die without you, Pelleas!" Lady Ettard sobbed.

"You too," Gawain said. "Come on, Terence.

146

Help me with this gear."

Thirty minutes later, fully armoured again, Gawain led Terence back out of Lady Ettard's castle and headed east, the sun lowering behind them.

"A more empty-headed woman I have never met," Gawain grunted after a moment. "If I had had to explain another joke—" He grimaced and looked at Terence. "You were lucky to get out when you did."

"Oh, lucky was I?" Terence demanded. "You forget I was with Sir Pelleas!"

Gawain laughed. "You're right, lad. You had your burden as well."

"Do you think they really will die, milord?" Terence asked.

"What, die for love?" Gawain considered this, then said, "If I've ever met two people stupid enough to do it, they would be the ones."

They rode side by side into their shadows while the long day ended.

9

NIMUE

Gawain and Terence did not stop until after dark. A full moon lit their way alongside farms and fields, back into the forest. Gawain rode with a still, thoughtful quietness. After about an hour, he muttered, half to himself, "A stupid and cruel woman. Who would have thought that such spite could lie behind such beauty?"

Terence was not sure if Gawain expected an answer, but after a moment Terence said, "I . . . I don't care for beautiful women, myself."

"What?" Gawain asked, half laughing, half shocked.

"I just mean the ones that I've met. I'm thinking of that woman who hated Abelleus and Lady Alisoun and Lady Ettard and your Aunt Morgan and . . . and women like that." Terence had been thinking mostly of the woman whose beautiful, cold face he had seen in the pond and whose fierce eyes still haunted his dreams, but he said nothing of her. "But . . . but I haven't known as many women as you, milord," he added.

Gawain rode in silence for a moment, his eyes on Terence's shadowed face. At last he said, "Morgan's not so bad, but I see what you mean." A moment later, he laughed softly and said, "You may have had some advantages growing up with a hermit." A few hours later, Gawain stopped by a lake, and without bothering to eat they rolled up in their blankets and let the soft lake sounds murmur them to sleep.

There had been no lakes in the Gentle Wood, where Terence had lived with the hermit, so the next morning he was surprised and enraptured by the misty, dreamy feel of a lake in the early morning. The air smelled cleaner, and Terence took long, slow breaths, letting the cool stillness fill his breast. A vague shape, like a person, appeared in the fog. Terence stood and watched the shape approach. His hair tingled, but he was not afraid. The shape seemed to bow, then point across the lake. Then it dissolved in the mist. A moment later, other shapes appeared, some like people, some like animals, and Terence smiled to them and nodded a greeting. When at last he looked away, Gawain was sitting up in his blankets, watching.

"What did you see, Terence?" Gawain asked quietly.

Terence hesitated. "Maybe nothing, milord. It just seemed that there were shapes in the mist. Did you see them?"

"Not I," Gawain replied. He raised one eyebrow and added, "Most people would have been afraid of shapes that appeared in the mist."

"Oh no, milord. These were friendly," Terence assured him.

Gawain looked at Terence searchingly, but he said nothing else. Terence prepared breakfast, and after they had eaten, Gawain said abruptly, "I can't make you out, Terence. Have you no idea who your parents were?"

"No, milord," Terence said. "I asked Trevisant one time, but of course he didn't know, seeing time backwards, the way he does. But he said I didn't need to know."

"He was wrong," Gawain said. "A boy should know his parents. Good or bad, they are a part of him."

Terence stirred the coals for a moment, then looked into Gawain's eyes. "I think so, too. Would you . . . tell me about your parents, milord?"

Gawain frowned, as if angry, and Terence was sorry he had asked. To his surprise, however, Gawain finally answered. "My father, King Lot, was a great soldier, a master with every weapon. When we were at peace, he would teach me." Gawain paused. "But we weren't at peace often, especially in late years. That was my mother's doing.

"My mother is named Morgause, from an ancient and magical and proud family." Gawain smiled faintly. "You wouldn't like her, Terence, because she's very beautiful. More beautiful than anyone, I think. My father worshipped her and did whatever she asked. When she sent him to war against Arthur, he died for her."

"She's still alive, then?"

"I don't know. When my father died, she disappeared without a word, not even to her children. She never did love us, I suppose. I don't imagine I ever really loved her either, but when I was a child I used to think I did."

Gawain sat in brooding silence, staring into the coals, and Terence left him alone. Indeed, Terence left Gawain alone quite a lot for the next few days in the lakeside camp. Gawain showed no desire to continue questing. He fished, but inattentively, and often let a good catch escape. One evening after a meal of trout, caught by Terence, and wild carrots, Gawain asked suddenly, "If beautiful women are cruel and hateful, what would you say about ugly women, Terence?"

"Me, milord?" Terence asked.

"Come now, Terence. I was expecting some word of wisdom from you. After all, you're the one who dislikes beautiful women, aren't you?"

"Only the ones I've met, milord."

"Well, what about the ugly women you've met?"

"I don't know any ugly—" Terence began.

"What about the hag at the feast?" demanded Gawain.

Terence hesitated. "I couldn't really say, milord. She . . . she wasn't very polite to you."

"Nor I to her. Would you say she was cruel?"

"No, milord. I think she was friendly."

Gawain frowned. "Like your shapes in the mist were friendly?"

Terence thought for a moment. "Just like that," he said.

The next morning when they woke, they were not alone. On a stone next to the lake sat a tall, willowy lady, swirling her bare feet in the waters. Behind her, a shining white horse cropped grass. The woman had straight black hair that hung to her waist. Her gown was white with a silvery sheen to it, gathered at the waist by a simple green girdle. Her face was not memorable in its features, but it shone with elegance, kindness and wisdom. Terence thought he could look at her forever.

Gawain sat upright among his blankets. "Good morning, madam," he said.

"Good morning, Sir Gawain," the woman said, smiling. "And good morning, Terence."

"Good . . . good morning, ma'am," Terence stammered.

"If I might ask," Gawain said, "how do you know our names?"

"I've come to find you," she replied. "Or you have come to find me, which in our world is almost the same thing."

"What world is that, madam?" Gawain asked, standing.

"The Other World," she said, still smiling. "I am Nimue, the Lady of the Lake."

Gawain bowed, his eyes alight. "I have heard of you, my lady."

Terence had never heard of the Lady of the Lake, but he too bowed deeply.

"No, no, Terence." Nimue laughed, and her laugh was like water splashing on stones. "You're

153

bowing to me as you would bow to royalty – or a god. Really, I'm not that different from you."

Terence straightened. "I'm sorry, my lady."

After a moment Gawain asked, "And why have you come to find us, my lady?"

"My mistress sent me. You have left some business undone, Sir Gawain," Nimue said.

"Pelleas and Ettard?" She nodded. "What can anyone do?" Gawain asked. "They are fools."

"Oh yes, lamentably so. But must fools be unhappy?"

"If they are unhappy, they have brought it on themselves," Gawain said.

"Have they?"

Gawain flushed slightly, but he said, "Perhaps my coming did not help them, but I made nothing worse. They were unhappy before I ever arrived in their land."

Nimue said nothing for a moment, then spoke gently. "You mean that in their place *you* would have been unhappy. But, as you say, your efforts helped no one."

Gawain's frown deepened. "But can I help them now?"

"I hope so. Come, let us go."

The ride back to Lady Ettard's castle was long, but the Lady of the Lake was a delightful companion. For over an hour, she talked with Terence about herbs and spices. She taught him about the curative powers of healing herbs like foxglove, woundwort, vervain and feverfew. As they drew near to Sir Pelleas's castle, Gawain said, "I still don't know what to do when I arrive."

"What do you think, Terence?" Nimue asked. "Have you any thoughts on what Sir Gawain should do?"

Glancing furtively at his master, Terence said, "No, my lady. I understand animals. They act in ways a body can predict. But people are different. I would have to know more about Sir Pelleas and Lady Ettard before I could guess how to help them."

Nimue smiled and nodded. Gawain rode in silence for a moment, then grumbled, "Very well. I shall try to think like an idiot."

Nimue sighed softly and stopped near a stand of trees. "Here," she said. "Pelleas is in this copse."

"Here? What the devil is he— Oh, I see. There's a hermitage or anchorage in there, and he's stretched out to die." Nimue nodded. "Thickwit," Gawain muttered to himself.

Behind the little grove of sycamores was a tiny cottage with a thatched roof. A rough cross stood in front of it. Gawain dismounted and stepped inside. About fifteen minutes later, Gawain reappeared in the doorway, disgust on his face. "I offered to help, but he thinks he'd rather die, thank you," he said.

"Sir Gawain," Nimue said, "it ill befits you to laugh at someone else's love, however foolish it might be. There is no love that might not appear ridiculous to someone else. Are you so sure that you will never love foolishly?"

Gawain blinked, then said, "I beg your pardon. I'll try again."

Terence heard their voices again, then a solid thump, and Gawain appeared in the doorway, carrying Sir Pelleas across his shoulders. "He changed his mind," he said.

"Sir Gawain, if this is how you plan to handle this affair, I'll wash my hands of you," Nimue protested. "What will you do if Ettard doesn't listen? Knock her over the head, too?"

Gawain grinned. "It *is* a temptation, but no. I just thought Pelleas might listen to me more in Ettard's presence."

Nimue shook her head wearily. About twenty minutes later, still several miles from Ettard's castle, Sir Pelleas, whom they had tied behind Terence's saddle, began to stir. "Villain," he muttered thickly. He looked at Terence, not recognizing him, and Terence pointed at Gawain, riding nearby. "Scoundrel," Sir Pelleas said.

"Terribly sorry, Pelleas," Gawain said. "But I can't let you dwindle away and die in there."

"Why not?" Sir Pelleas asked in a muffled voice.

"Well, I can't help feeling partly responsible for—" Gawain began.

"Partly? When you've traduced me to the woman whom I thought I loved? When you've defiled a fair lady? When you've ravished a vessel of purity?"

"Here now," Gawain protested, "all I did was kiss her. And I promise you, I didn't even enjoy it."

Sir Pelleas went into a fit, mouthing terrible curses and wrenching his body right and left. In a pained voice, Nimue said, "I don't think that was very helpful, Sir Gawain."

"Sorry," he muttered.

In his frenzy, Sir Pelleas slid face first off of Terence's horse into the dirt. Stifling an oath, Gawain dismounted and helped Pelleas up. "Look, Pelleas, I'm trying to help you," Gawain said.

"Help me? By kissing the woman who was my Heart, my Purest Love?"

"What is a kiss? It's nothing!"

"Nothing to you, perhaps. To me, it was everything! How would you like to see another man kissing the woman you loved?"

For several seconds Gawain stared into the distance, then said, "You're right, Pelleas. I should never have kissed her. I'm sorry. But it was all part of a plan. You were *supposed* to come in and stop me. I was pretending."

Sir Pelleas grunted. "And was she pretending when she kissed you back?" He took a deep breath, then said, "I suppose I should thank you for showing me how false is the Lady – lady! Ha! – the Lady Ettard. Now I can lay aside that misplaced love I once held."

"Then you don't love her anymore?" Gawain asked.

"I don't feel anything at all for that woman."

Gawain said, "Well, don't you think you ought to show her that?"

"At last you've said something worth saying, Sir Gawain," Nimue said quietly.

Sir Pelleas nodded slowly. "You're right. She should know the result of her perfidy. I could show her disdain, treat her with a . . . a cold politeness. And then," he added, warming to his theme, "I'll show affection for another lady! *Then* she'll be sorry! I'll do it! I will!"

At Lady Ettard's castle, the guards threw open the gates as soon as the riders approached. Nimue said, "Lady Ettard is not well, I believe. I think the guards must hope that we can help her."

They left their horses in the courtyard and followed Nimue to the garden, where Lady Ettard and Gawain had kissed. There, on a richly draped canopy bed that had been set under a chestnut tree, the Lady Ettard languished. She was pale, and her left hand held a small vinaigrette, which she was sniffing when the four visitors entered. She sat up as if pricked with a needle and gasped, "Pelleas! My love! You've come back!"

At first Sir Pelleas looked at her almost tenderly, but after she had spoken, he sneered and replied, "Yes, I've come back, but only to look with scorn on the falsest of fair maidens in all this vain world."

Lady Ettard moaned and fell back on her pillows, clutching feebly at her vinaigrette. "I thought . . . I thought perhaps you still loved me!"

"Ha!" Sir Pelleas barked harshly. "You are right that I loved you once. You were a pure woman once! You resisted the advances of men! But then you threw yourself into this knave's arms, and put aside your maidenly innocence! I despise you now, who once despised me!"

Gawain asked, "Was it maidenly of her to empty the kitchen swill over your head?"

"Kitchen swill! That was nothing! Once she had me tied to a long board and had two burly servants sweep her stables with me!"

Lady Ettard showed a stir of interest. She said, "That was just after the time that I fed you the slop that the hogs left."

"No no, it was the time before," Sir Pelleas said impatiently. "Just after the Christmas feast."

"Of course! When I harnessed you with my pony and you pulled my sleigh!"

"And all your curses only proved your virtue and gave me opportunity to prove the constancy of my love. But now," Sir Pelleas said harshly, "you have proven yourself a straw-damsel of the worst type! A careless courtesan! A painted paramour!"

Lady Ettard burst into wailing tears, and following his plan to make Lady Ettard jealous, Sir Pelleas turned to one of the servant girls and began complimenting her extravagantly. The girl tried to edge away, but he followed her with his effusive praise. Lady Ettard burst into louder, more pathetic sobs. Gawain whispered to Nimue for a moment. She looked startled, but she nodded, and Gawain moved back next to Terence. "Watch this, lad," he whispered.

Taking a deep breath and setting her face into an expression of deep scorn, the gentle Nimue strode over to Sir Pelleas, turned him roughly around to face her, and slapped him loudly on the cheek. He stared at her, stunned. "You worm!" she shouted. "You abuser of womanhood! How dare you say such things about this gentlewoman? Who but you sent this same knave Gawain to this woman?" Sir Pelleas's jaw dropped, and his eyes grew round. Nimue looked furiously at him for a moment, then stuck her tongue out at him and resumed her tirade.

"On your knees, you canker, you plague, you boil! Kneel and beg for my forgiveness, and then, if I feel you are worthy, I will kick you over to this fine lady's bed to beg her forgiveness as well. Do you hear me? Kneel!"

Sir Pelleas dropped to his knees as if he had been hit with a log. Reverently he gazed into Nimue's face. "Indeed I beg your pardon, my lady! I should be shot for uttering such words before thy chaste ears! Tell me, I beg of thee, what is thy name, O worshipful goddess!"

Nimue started, then looked helplessly back at Gawain. Gawain covered his eyes and groaned, "Good Gog, the sod's gone and fallen in love with Nimue!"

"I . . . I won't tell you," Nimue said. "You don't

deserve it."

Pelleas smiled dreamily and said, "I shall call you
. . . Clorinda! Or Phoebe! I shall write sonnets to
your purity, your innocence!" Nimue stared.

Gawain swore softly. "Now I have to rescue her,
too," he groaned. He stepped forward, but Terence
grabbed Gawain's arm.

"Wait, milord!" he whispered hoarsely. "Look at
Ettard!"

While Nimue had been abusing Sir Pelleas, Lady
Ettard had stopped sobbing. Now, pale and weak,
she was crawling out of bed, a ferocious look in her
eyes. "You!" she gasped. "You! Pelleas! You fickle,
good-for-naught, unstable, brainless whelp! How
dare you accuse me of being faithless, when you
throw yourself at the feet of the first shrewish
wench who'll curse you as you deserve!" She sat
unsteadily on the edge of the bed.

Sir Pelleas gazed bemusedly at her, then stared
up at Nimue, then back at Lady Ettard,
consternation on his face. "But you . . . but Ettard
. . . you . . . and this virtuous lady here . . ." He
gabbled incoherently.

Heaving a huge sigh of relief, Nimue smiled
and turned to Lady Ettard. "Now you stop
abusing this fine knight," she said. "There's
nothing wrong with loving a different lady now

162

and then!"

"Oh, yes there is!" Ettard gritted her teeth. "Love must be eternal!"

"It's true," Sir Pelleas agreed, looking plaintively at Nimue. "I swore eternal love for Ettard. And now . . . oh, what have I done?"

"You've done nothing to be punished for," Nimue said firmly.

"Well, he shall be!" Lady Ettard announced, standing up tall. Weak as she was, though, her legs could not support her weight, and she fell face first onto the neat gravel garden path. Forgetting all about Nimue, Sir Pelleas scampered toward her on all fours.

"My dove! My heart! Are you hurt?"

"You stay away from me!" Lady Ettard spluttered, her face still in the dirt. Slowly she climbed into a sitting position. She threw one disdainful look toward Nimue, then turned all of her fulminating gaze on Sir Pelleas. "Don't you come an inch closer, you maggot, or I'll have you stepped on and fed to the sparrows! You . . . you—" Filled with emotion she clutched a handful of gravel and began throwing small stones at Sir Pelleas.

"Oh my dearest life!" Sir Pelleas cried. "You know I could never love any soul but – ouch! – but you. I never really loved that – ow! – that woman who was here! My every nerve strains – ouch! – to behold you!"

"Behold this, insect!" Lady Ettard shouted, throwing harder and faster.

"I've written a sonnet to your nose my dearest heart! Ouch! It goes *'J'entends de la'*— ouch!"

Nimue had slipped away from the scene, joining Gawain and Terence. "Well done, after all, Sir Gawain," she said. "At last they are happy again."

"Nauseating," he said, shaking his head slowly.

"Shall we go? I have some instructions to help you on your quest now that you have passed this test."

"Yes, let's," Gawain said, "quickly." The Lady of the Lake led Gawain back into the castle, and Terence followed. As he stepped into Lady Ettard's stateroom, he took a last look behind him. Lady Ettard still sat in the gravel, throwing pebbles at Sir Pelleas, who cowered only two yards away, still doggedly reciting his French sonnet to her.

"Brundle!" Lady Ettard shouted. "Bring me more stones! Bigger ones!"

10

GANSCOTTER'S CASTLE

They rode unchallenged out of Lady Ettard's castle, back into the eastern forest. As they entered the shadows, Nimue asked, "Sir Gawain? How did you know what to do?"

"I almost didn't." He laughed. "When that dafthead in there turned his puppy eyes at you, I thought I had *really* ruined things."

Nimue smiled ruefully. "So did I, for a moment. Sometimes it is a compliment to be admired. Other times it is an insult."

"And yet Pelleas thrives on insults," Gawain said. "I only understood that when he and Ettard began to reminisce about his different humiliations."

"And Ettard? On what does she thrive?" Nimue asked.

Gawain considered this. "At first I thought that she wanted a forceful, dominating lover – I believe she thought so, too. But what she really wanted was to control, not to be controlled."

"Remember that, Sir Gawain," Nimue said. "Not even a very foolish woman like Ettard wishes to be controlled."

"I will remember," Gawain said, watching Nimue curiously.

They arrived at their lakeside camp in the middle of the afternoon. Gawain stretched wearily and started to dismount, but Nimue stopped him.

"I'm sorry, Sir Gawain, Terence. But you are not finished today."

"Ah," Gawain said. "You said you would give us further instructions for our quest."

She nodded. "These are the last instructions you will receive: follow me into the lake, and then follow the lake itself. Follow the lake until the candle of heaven shows you an open door. Enter there, and you will face your final test."

"Final test for what? What is it that I'm being tested to achieve?" Gawain asked, frowning. "What is this quest that you and Terence's messenger and Morgan keep on about?"

"Sometimes, Sir Gawain, the goal of a quest is to understand the goal of the quest."

Gawain sighed. "I suppose you Other Worlders have to talk like that. I wonder if you mean to explain something or to conceal it."

"Both." Nimue smiled, turning her white horse toward the lake. "Follow me. And mind that you neither rest nor leave the waters until you have arrived at the door." She rode into the lake, and Terence and Gawain followed. Nimue repeated, "Follow the lake," and then sank, horse and all, beneath the surface. Not a ripple showed that she had ever been there.

They both stared at the smooth surface for a long moment. Then Gawain said, "Come on, Terence. 'Follow the lake,' she said, which I suppose means to follow the shore."

Gawain started splashing through the shallows along the shore, but Terence did not move. Suddenly, unprompted, he thought of the shape that had appeared in the morning mist that day, the vaguely human figure that had pointed across the lake. "No, milord," he said.

Gawain stopped and looked back over his shoulder, "What, lad?"

"I . . . I think we should go that way," Terence pointed straight across the lake.

"On horseback?" Gawain asked mildly. "We'll drown."

"I don't know, milord. I just know that following the shoreline is wrong."

Gawain looked at Terence thoughtfully. "Can you say how you know?" Terence shook his head. "But you know it all the same?" Gawain continued. Terence nodded, feeling very foolish. Gawain pursed his lips, then, with a crooked smile, said, "I suppose that's good enough for me. Lead the way, Terence."

Terence looked across the lake, wondered briefly how it felt to drown, and urged his mount into motion. His horse had to begin swimming almost at once, and Terence slipped off the saddle and paddled alongside to lighten the animal's load. After a few seconds, though, Terence's horse stopped swimming and scrambled onto a submerged sand bar. Terence put his feet down carefully and found himself in chest-deep water.

"Look, milord! It's shallower here. That's lucky!"

Guingalet climbed onto the shallow spot, and Gawain said, "Lucky."

Straight across the lake they headed, always in shallows no higher than their horses' bellies. Terence walked ahead, holding his horse's reins, feeling with his feet for holes and deep water. Gawain, heavy in his armour, stayed on

Guingalet's back, watching Terence press ahead.

Once, Terence veered a few feet to the right and felt the ground slip away under his feet. He splashed to the surface, gasping. "So it's deep just to the right, is it?" Gawain said. "Try a few steps to the left, Terence." Terence did, and again felt the bottom slope downward. "Don't you see, Terence?" Gawain said. "We're on an underwater road. From up here you can see it. On either side, the water is dark, but right ahead it's lighter."

Terence saw. Ahead stretched a thin ribbon of lighter-coloured water, where the lake was shallow. "Who would build an underwater road, milord?" he asked.

"And why?" Gawain added.

They plodded on. Now that they could see their way, Terence no longer needed to walk, and he remounted and followed the pale path. The shore behind them grew more distant, but the far shore never seemed to grow nearer.

And then the fog fell, or rather rose, because it seemed to spring up from the lake itself. One minute Terence had been able to see all the shores of the lake, and the next he could barely make out the faint outline of his own horse's ears.

Terence dismounted and led his horse again, holding to the reins as to a lifeline, calling directions back to Gawain. More times than he could count he stepped off the road into the deep water and had to pull himself out by the reins. Once Guingalet slipped on the edge, and only by a superb bit of horsemanship did Gawain stay on the road. All around, tiny splashing noises began to come to Terence's ears. He stopped. "Milord?"

"I hear them, boy."

Something long and cold slithered past Terence's leg. "Milord!" he shouted. "There's something there! By my leg!"

"Terence, don't move! Not a muscle! Do you hear me!" Gawain said quietly. "There are thousands of them. If we try to escape, we'll both end up at the bottom of the lake."

Something like a long snake or an eel slithered up Terence's leg, over his shoulder, and back into the water. "We can't stop, milord. Nimue said we mustn't." Terence took a deep breath. "I'll move slowly."

Terence whispered to his horse, which twitched convulsively, and began to move along the road again. For fully fifteen minutes he put one foot ahead of the other while the creatures swirled and writhed and coiled around him. His arms ached from holding his horse's reins tight. One creature coiled three times around his waist, and Terence broke into a feverish sweat, but he still stepped forward, giving directions to Gawain in a hoarse whisper. No sound met his ears but the faint splashes of the things sliding in and out of the water. Behind him, he heard Gawain mutter, "And to think I almost had Gaheris as squire." Terence felt braver and stepped forward again.

The fog grew somehow darker and began to gather itself into shapes around him. First there was a bull, head lowered, then a human shape, then others. They flitted and shifted before Terence's eyes, not greeting him in friendship as had the figures in the morning mist, but sneering and scowling at him. And still the creatures under the water coiled and twisted around his legs. Terence could scarcely breathe, but he set his mind on putting one foot ahead of the next. A few yards ahead, two wraiths took the shapes of a lady and a knight. Terence stopped and caught his breath.

"What is it, Terence?" Gawain whispered.

"Nothing, milord." Terence choked and stepped forward again. Now he heard the lady's voice, muttering softly. Terence took another step, and the lady's voice grew clearer.

"Not now. No, not now. Not while Merlin is still with him. But it will be soon. Merlin will leave, and then—" Terence clenched his teeth and stepped closer. The female shape whirled around and saw him. "You! Again!" Terence stepped forward, missed the road, and plunged over his head in the lake, into the midst of the writhing sea creatures. Slowly he pulled himself out by his horse's reins, slippery beasts coiling and dripping from his shoulders.

"Terence!" Gawain whispered urgently.

"Here, milord," Terence gasped. "I'm alive." The shapes of the lady and the knight were gone. Terence began to cry from fear and weariness, but he stretched out his foot and began walking again.

At last the splashes of the coiling creatures grew fainter. For a long moment, neither spoke, then Gawain said, "I'll dream about that for the rest of my life."

Terence breathed deeply and splashed water on his face to wash away his tears. "Do you know what they are?" he asked.

"They can only have been shaughuses, lad. Poison eels. I've heard they have only to run their tongues over your skin to kill you instantly."

Terence felt faint, but he took another step. "To the right a bit, milord," he said.

About an hour later the fog lifted, but they could see no better than before. The sun had set, and a thick cloud blotted the moonlight. The air was fresh, and the breeze was cool. Gawain swore to himself.

"What, milord?"

"Thunderstorm coming. And here we are in a lake, the worst place to be." Then, to himself, he added, "And me in full armour."

A flash of lightning lit the horizon, and a few seconds later thunder boomed around them. Then came another flash and rumble, and then the sky opened and poured itself out on them. Torrents of hard rain beat against them, and all around them lightning flashed. Terence trudged on through the night, shouting his directions to Gawain sometimes two or three times before he heard an answering shout. A huge lightning bolt seemed to dance over their heads, and in its light Terence saw with amazement that there were trees on both sides of him.

"Milord! Milord!" he shouted.

"I see, Terence! We're in a river now! We must have—" His voice disappeared in a crash of thunder. The river current swept Terence from his feet, but he held the reins and pulled himself to the surface, just as lightning burst beside them. The sound hit Terence like a blow, and it was followed immediately by a second explosion to his right. At once he could see everything, in the fierce glow of a lightning-struck pine that sent long, roaring flames toward the sky. Beside him, built right into the side of the river, rose a huge stone castle. The opposite bank, where the tree burned, was only a few yards away. As he watched, a mighty drawbridge lowered from the castle to rest on the far shore.

"That's it, Terence! The door!" Gawain shouted. "Up the bank!"

Dazed, Terence followed Gawain's example, pulling and shouting and begging his mount until both horses stood dripping on dry land. Gawain grasped Terence's shoulder. "Good lad! Now, into the castle!"

They led their horses across the drawbridge into a large entry hall, lit by cheery torches stuck in the wall. The drawbridge closed behind them, and the raging storm suddenly seemed a thousand miles away. "Well, we're here," Gawain said. The lines on his face were carved deep with weariness. "The candle of heaven showed us the door. Wherever here is."

"Welcome, travellers," said a bright, pleasant female voice. "Your chambers are waiting. Would you like separate bedchambers or would you prefer to share one?" A fair-haired girl appeared around a corner, carrying a lamp in each hand.

Gawain stared at her for a second, then bowed.

"One bedchamber, please," he said.

"Very well. Follow me, please." She turned and walked gracefully down a long hallway. "The grooms will see to your horses. The Master and his daughter will see you in the morning after you have breakfasted. One of the servants will bring you your breakfast in your room. Warm water is awaiting you, and your fire is lit."

Gawain shot Terence a helpless look, then said, "We've come this far, lad. Let's go." They left their sodden horses and followed the girl.

"If I can do anything else for your comfort," she was saying, "please let me or one of the other servants know."

"You could answer a few questions," Gawain said.

"I am at your service, Sir Gawain," she nodded, turning into a darker hallway.

"First, how do you know my name, and how did you know we would be arriving?"

"When you meet the Master, you will no longer wonder how he knows what he knows," she said with a patient smile.

"Who is the Master, then?" Gawain asked.

"He is Ganscotter the Enchanter," she said.

"An enchanter?" Gawain repeated.

"*The* Enchanter," she replied.

"Not so long ago I was with the great Merlin—" Gawain began.

"Even Merlin, Sir Gawain, is a servant of greater ones," the girl said. "Here is your room. If you think of anything you need, simply pull that rope, and it shall be brought to you. Sleep well, Sir Gawain. Pleasant dreams, Terence."

The girl left, taking both lamps with her. The only light in the room came from the fire roaring in the hearth. Near the hearth were two chairs, and just behind them two huge old beds. Beside each bed was a small table on which were laid out several towels, a pitcher of water, and a change of clothing. Terence and Gawain washed and fell thankfully into their beds to sleep like the dead until morning.

Terence awoke to the sound of a gentle tapping. He opened his eyes and saw Gawain, dressed in a magnificent green brocade blouse, rise from the chair next to the fire and cross the room to open the door. A plump kitchenmaid stood there, beaming and holding a heavy tray piled high with ham and bacon and savoury rolls and eggs and a pot of porridge and fresh apples and pears and plums and a good deal more. Terence sat upright in his bed, holding the blankets around him.

"The Master will receive you in one hour in his chambers," the maid said as soon as Gawain had taken the tray. "Lady Audrey will come and get you. You eat a good breakfast, now." She curtseyed and left.

An hour later the fair-haired lady who had shown them to their rooms came to get them. She led them through a bewildering series of halls, up a winding staircase, to the ramparts at the top of the castle.

"Terence, look at the river!" Gawain said suddenly.

Terence looked over the wall, but there was no river. The only water that was visible was the moat that surrounded the castle. "It's not there, milord," Terence said faintly.

"Look there," Gawain said. He pointed at a lightning-blasted pine, still smoking beside the moat.

Then Terence understood and whispered, "That's the tree that we saw last night. We came out of the moat, didn't we?"

"Looks that way," Gawain said. He turned to their guide and said, "Lady Audrey, is it?" She stopped and looked politely at them. "We came out of your moat last night, but I see no streams leading to it. Can you tell us how we got there?"

She smiled pleasantly and said, "All the waters of your world are contained in our moat, Sir Gawain. Come. The Master is waiting." They followed the lady along the ramparts to a tower that took up all of one corner of the castle. Without knocking, she pushed open a massive door, and they entered a simply furnished room with a thick carpet on the floor and a few tapestries on the wall. In the centre of the room a small man with a pleasant smile and a curly brown beard sat on a throne carved in dark wood.

"Welcome, Sir Gawain!" the man said, rising. He looked around thirty-five, but something in his eyes was far older than that. "And welcome, Terence!" the man said, turning glowing eyes on Terence. "You have done well. I have high hopes that you will achieve your tasks."

They both bowed deeply, and Gawain said, "Sir, so too do I, though I know not what my task might be."

"This is your goal, Sir Gawain," the man said. He reached around his wooden throne and withdrew a long sash in cloth of gold. On the sash were embroidered the words "The Maiden's Knight."

"I am to become The Maiden's Knight?" Gawain asked. "What is that?"

"One whose task is to defend the fairer sex with courage and honour and with – discrimination."

"Sir, you speak of a burden, not a prize."

The man nodded. "Sir Gawain, you will come to understand that the greatest boons given in our world are burdens. In your world men fight for glory; it is not so here." He gazed mistily at the walls for a moment, then looked back at Gawain and Terence. "I, as you know, am Ganscotter the Enchanter, the lord of this castle and much, much more – a ruler among the faeries, and a humble servant of my own master. I am also a great admirer of yours, Sir Gawain. I have watched your adventures since you were a child, and I should like to hear the tale of your most recent quest. Will you tell it?"

Gawain blinked and said, "Do you not know what has happened, sir? I would have thought that you knew the events better than I."

"I know the events, Sir Gawain. I wish to hear the tale. There is a difference."

Slowly at first but then more easily, Gawain began to tell all that had happened since they left King Arthur's court in search of the hart. He assumed no false modesty when recounting his triumphs, but neither did he pass over his failures. He told of his own surliness toward Terence on the day of their departure, and he spoke openly of his anger and lack of mercy toward Alardin and Ablamor and of his accidental slaying of Ablamor's wife. He spoke briefly of Alisoun and Pelleas and Ettard, and at great length of Terence's courage in leading the way through the lake, the night, the fog, the storm and the shaughuses.

When he was done, Ganscotter looked warmly at Terence, then turned back to Gawain and said, "Well told, Sir Gawain. Now I must ask you a question. You have been through many dangers, and you have met many maidens. Tell me what you have learned of women."

Gawain hesitated. "I dare not speak, my lord. I have learned above all that I still have much to learn. I must allow women the privilege of interpreting themselves as they will."

"You are either very wise or very diplomatic, Sir Gawain," a rich, low voice said from the other side of the room. "Whichever is the case, you have answered well."

His face stricken, Gawain leaped to his feet and whirled around. There, in the doorway, stood the hag from the feast.

"My daughter," Ganscotter said. "Lorie."

Hesitantly, Gawain took several steps toward the ugly woman. Then he knelt in front of her and said, "I have hoped that I would see you again, my lady."

"Have you?" she asked. Her soft voice sent a thrill through Terence, and Gawain quivered visibly. "Why is that, Sir Gawain?"

"To beg your forgiveness, my lady. I was unpardonably rude to you, but I ask your pardon all the same."

"It is well said," Lorie answered. "To forgive the unforgivable is the breath of life in this world. You are forgiven, Sir Gawain. It is to your credit, too, that you do not mention that I deliberately provoked your rudeness."

"I did not think that provocation was an excuse, my lady."

"There is no such thing as an excuse, Sir Gawain," she said laughing, and her laughter was like the wind, the water and a thousand songbirds singing together. "Stand up, Gawain," she said. "It is not right that you should kneel to me." Gawain stood, his eyes still on Lorie's face. "And now I must meet Terence," Lorie said, crossing the room to the squire. "I understand that you have served your master well, Terence. I am pleased."

Terence gulped and said, "Thank you, my lady."

"No, Terence. Do not call me 'my lady.' You must call me Lorie."

"Yes, my lady," Terence stammered.

"All in good time, my child." Ganscotter smiled.

Gawain and Terence spent the rest of the day with their host and hostess, and never had Terence known greater contentment. Ganscotter, though his ancient eyes remained awe-inspiring, was a gentle companion. A peaceful, dreamlike bliss stole over Terence when Ganscotter spoke, and he felt brave and able to do anything. While Gawain and Lorie talked and laughed by the fire, Ganscotter took Terence out onto the castle ramparts.

"Do you like my daughter?" the enchanter asked suddenly.

"I think so, sir," Terence said. "You are an enchanter, but she . . . she does not seem to be an enchantress."

"You can tell, can't you? No, Lorie is not an enchantress. At least not the sort of enchantress you mean." Terence glanced quickly at Ganscotter's face. "Yes, I know about the one you saw in the pond," the enchanter said. "Indeed, that was The Enchantress herself."

"*The* Enchantress, sir? Who is she?"

"She has a different name in every age. But in every age she appears, always with the same goal:

to rule as queen over the world of men."

"How can she do that?"

"First she must remove the world's kings and princes. We shall soon see if the Enchantress of this age will succeed. Tell me, child," he said, in a lighter tone, "do you like serving as Sir Gawain's squire?"

"Yes, sir. Very much."

"Is it not too humble a position for you?"

Terence was puzzled. "No, sir. Really it is more exalted than I ever thought to be. I do not know my parents, but—"

"Do you not?" Ganscotter asked.

"No, sir," Terence said. "And there is no one to tell me. Unless—" A sudden hope brightened his eyes, "Sir, do you know who my parents are?"

Ganscotter nodded and spoke gently. "Yes, child. Your mother was a village maiden with laughter in her eyes, and your father was a traveller from this world who saw her and loved her. I cannot explain to you how one from the faery lands can love and give himself to an earthbound daughter of men, but it happens. You were born and gave joy to both your parents. But in that world joy has an end, and your mother died while you were a baby. She was weak from illness, but she held you in her arms as she died, and her eyes still smiled. Her eyes were very like yours."

Ganscotter paused, and his face grew sad. "But a child born to the world of men cannot come to our world to stay, and so you were given to one who could be trusted."

"But I've come to your world now," Terence said.

"Ah, it is a different matter now that you are grown. The faeries never forget their own."

Tears warmed Terence's eyes, then his cheeks. "Thank you, sir," he said gruffly. "I have wanted to know that my mother loved me." Terence peeked through his tears at the enchanter, then took courage and said, "And my father? Is he—? Will I—?"

"Your father loves you as well," Ganscotter said. "More than that you must not ask now."

"But why not? When can I know?"

Ganscotter frowned. "When it is time, Terence. For now, you will have to trust me."

"Yes, sir. I'm sorry, sir."

Ganscotter waited a moment, then said gently, "I believe you have some skill with herbs. Would you like to see my gardens?"

The wonderful day finally drew to a close, and after dinner in Ganscotter's chambers and hours of comfortable conversation around the table,

Terence and Gawain were left in their own warm room. Peace filling his breast, Terence lay on his bed and watched the firelight make merry shadows on the wall. From the darkest corner of the room came a faint stirring. Gawain and Terence both turned quickly and gazed into the blackness. A tall human shadow stood there.

"Gawain?" There was no mistaking Lorie's voice.

"Yes, Lorie?" Gawain's voice sounded oddly strained.

"Do you know why I am here?"

"I am not sure," he said faintly.

She said simply, "I have come to offer you my love."

Gawain was silent for a long – very long – minute. Then he said, "I accept it. And I give you mine."

Lorie stepped out of the shadows into the firelight, and Terence stared in astonishment. Gone were the scars on her cheeks, the blemishes, the long and crooked nose, the decaying teeth. In their place was a face of great grace and wisdom, with lips that smiled and eyes that saw far and deep. Gawain stared, dumbfounded.

"This is my other appearance, Gawain," she said. "Now you have seen me in two different faces. From this time forth I shall appear in only one. Which shall it be?"

Gawain blinked dazedly. "What?"

"You must choose which appearance I am to have. Choose, and I will obey."

Gawain gazed abstractedly at her and did not speak. Terence made no sound. He knew that he was not a part of this moment, but only a spectator. Gawain looked at Lorie for a minute, then another. She waited patiently. For a full ten minutes, Gawain looked at her. Then, to Terence's surprise, a tear appeared in Gawain's eye, ran down his cheek, hung quivering for a second on his beard, then splashed on his bare chest. In a voice that sounded as if it were wrenched out of his chest he said, "No, Lorie. I return the decision to you. Appear as you will. I will not command in this."

Lorie's face relaxed, and she sighed deeply. "Oh, Gawain," she said, "I prayed that you would be the one, my love. I choose this appearance."

And then Gawain took Lorie in his arms, and they held each other tenderly. Discreetly looking away from their embrace, Terence saw that Ganscotter had joined them – from where he did not know – and was standing against the wall smiling at the couple.

"You have passed your final test, my son," he

said. Gawain looked up, tears of joy glistening in his eyes, as Ganscotter moved toward him. Lorie stepped away from Gawain, and Gawain knelt before the enchanter. Solemnly, Ganscotter placed the gold sash of The Maiden's Knight over Gawain's head. "This is the mark of The Maiden's Knight, Sir Gawain. Wear it by your heart, beneath your armour. It is your gift and your burden. Now rise."

As he finished speaking, the room around them began to grow hazy and distant. In a few seconds, Ganscotter and Lorie and all their surroundings were gone, and Gawain and Terence and their horses stood in a meadow by a stream, shivering in a chill wind. Only by the golden sash across his master's chest, the dulcet voice whispering "Goodbye, my love" through the wind, and Gawain's wretched, grief-stricken sobs did Terence know that this dream had been true.

11

GALATINE

Gawain wept into the night while Terence stood guard over his master. The wind was frigid, and Terence could tell there would be frost in the morning. The horses huddled together, and Terence spread both Gawain's blankets and his own over his master's shaking form. Finally, exhausted by sorrow, Gawain slept, and Terence paced back and forth to keep warm, miserable but determined not to disturb his lord's rest.

At dawn, Gawain stirred. Terence could see the moment when the memory of Lorie returned to him, because his face grew suddenly bleak. Terence looked away. He had gathered wood and kindling, and as soon as Gawain moved he began to build a fire. He did not speak. Gawain examined the blankets and frowned.

188

"This is your blanket, Terence," he said.

"I wasn't sleepy, milord."

"You're a liar," Gawain said, "but thank you." He breathed deeply for a moment, then shook himself and stood. "What the devil is wrong with the weather? It's never this cold in midsummer."

"It's not summer, milord," Terence said. "Look at the leaves."

In the growing eastern light, sparse yellow and red and orange and gold leaves became visible one by one. "Autumn?" Gawain asked softly.

"October, milord. The ivy's in bloom."

"October? But it was—"

"Ay, milord. We entered Ganscotter's castle in July. Maybe we were there longer than we thought."

"Like King Herla," Gawain muttered.

"Who?"

"It's a children's story, lad. A king who went to visit the faeries for an evening, and when he came back hundreds of years had passed."

Terence looked up, alarmed. "You think—?"

"I don't know. At least three months have gone."

When they had eaten and warmed themselves at the fire, Terence felt much better. "Where to now, milord?" he asked.

"It's all one to me," Gawain said shortly. Terence

looked at his feet, stretched out toward the flames. In a moment Gawain said, "Sorry, Terence. I shouldn't take it out on you."

"I'll take what I'm given, milord," he said.

For the first time that morning, Gawain's bleak expression softened. He said, "Ah, now that's put me in my place. You're right, lad. So where to now? I don't know." Terence waited, not speaking. "All right, Terence," Gawain said finally. "What is it?"

"Well, milord, if it's really been three months – or at least three months, as you said – maybe we should look for the well where we're to meet Sir Marhault and Sir Tor. That was supposed to be in three months, wasn't it?"

Gawain nodded. "All right. Of course we may find that Sir Marhault and Tor died hundreds of years ago, but it's somewhere to go." He did not sound excited, but Terence was satisfied that they had something to do.

Having no idea which direction to take, they simply followed the stream. Gawain was silent, and Terence respected his mood. As the sun rose in the sky, Terence could see its strength infusing his master. At last, just before noon, Terence said, "Milord?"

"Yes, Terence?"

"When you let Lady Lorie choose her own

appearance, that was because you trusted her, wasn't it?"

Gawain thought for a moment, then said, "Partly. There's more than that, but that's a part of it."

"All right. Do you still love her, milord?" Terence asked.

At that Gawain sat up straight. Angrily he replied, "Do I still—? Terence, I love her more every second. Never ask that again, do you hear me?"

"All right. Do you trust her enough to believe she still loves you, too?"

Gawain looked sharply at Terence. "What the devil do you know about it, Terence?" he demanded irritably.

"Nothing, milord."

They rode in silence for another twenty minutes. Then Gawain said, "I have lost my lady. At least I still have my friend. Thank you, Terence."

Soon they found a path they recognized, and an hour later they rode into the clearing where they had met the Three Questing Ladies and found the others waiting. Sir Marhault and his lady, Sir Tor and Plogrun and the old lady, and even Lady Alisoun were there. Gawain bowed and said, "Good day, friends."

"I told you he'd make it!" Tor cried triumphantly. He strode forward and grasped Gawain's hand. "Only a week late, too! Hello, Terence. Gawain, your young lady – I say, do you always misplace ladies the same day you pick them up? – she thought you were probably dead. Come join our lunch!" He waved his hand at a picnic feast of bread and cheese.

Gawain smiled at Lady Alisoun and asked blandly, "And just how long did it take you to finish off that knight you rode off with?"

"I don't finish off my knights!" she snapped.

"My apologies," he said, bowing. "But he *is* dead, isn't he?"

"Yes," she said reluctantly. "But he died bravely!"

"I congratulate him," Gawain said. He turned to Tor and said, "You must tell me how your three months went, Tor. Adventures? Battles? Dragons? Giants?"

Tor laughed and said, "No no, it's old Marhault who's killed a giant. I've just done in a few knights and saved a lady. And what about you, Gawain?"

"Nothing to speak of." Gawain smiled. "Just dabbled in a few love affairs and been for a swim." His eyes held a distant, tender look, and Terence knew he was thinking of his love in the faery castle.

Tor looked disappointed, but he also saw Gawain's eyes, and he asked no other questions.

They ate well in the shade of a towering oak. Sir Marhault and Tor told Gawain their stories carefully, but already with the ease and fluency of frequent telling. Sir Marhault had crossed lances with a few other wandering knights, unseating them all, but the pinnacle of his quest was his defeat of a troublesome giant named Taulurd for the Earl Fergus in the lands of the north. It was surely a great victory, but Sir Marhault almost seemed to regret it. "The giant was a nuisance and truly had to be dealt with," he said, "but he had no more wit than a child, and he wept like a mother-less babe as he died."

Tor's story was simpler. Not only had he won a tournament, at which he unseated thirty knights, but a few days after that he had saved a beautiful lady, called the Lady of the Rock, from two brothers who were trying to take her land. He had fought them both at once and, though wounded slightly, had killed them. When he finished, Gawain said, "Unseated thirty knights, you say?"

"Yes," Tor said. "I don't mean to say that they were of your stature, or Marhault's, of course."

"Still, thirty knights is not bad. You must have improved a bit since I last saw you joust."

"Oh well, I practised a bit after we split up," Tor said vaguely. Plogrun snorted, and the Lady Lyne allowed herself a tiny smile. Later, Terence was to hear the full story from Plogrun, how the first two months of the quest Tor had spent in intensive training at Lady Lyne's home in the south, jousting and sparring with his sword and practising on horseback for eighteen to twenty hours a day. Lady Lyne, Terence gathered, was a hard taskmaster, and Plogrun's professional jealousy of her had made him work Tor as hard as she had. They must have been hellish months for the young knight, but from his successes in the last month of the quest it seemed they had been worth the pain.

When Tor finished his tale, everyone looked at Gawain. He told them briefly about Sir Pelleas and Lady Ettard, omitting all reference to Nimue. Then he said, "After that little episode, there is really nothing more to tell. We found ourselves at a large castle, where a gentleman and his daughter entertained us royally for what seemed but one evening and one day, but when we left we found that three months had gone by. That was last night. We came here immediately." He smiled apologetically and added, "Not a very interesting quest, I'm afraid."

"Three months went by in one night?" Tor asked skeptically.

"I have heard of such things," said the lady who had ridden with Sir Marhault. "You were enchanted."

Gawain smiled. "Perhaps I still am," he said.

Plogrun looked suspiciously at Terence. "Right, lad," he whispered. "What really happened?"

Terence blinked innocently and said, "What do you mean?" Plogrun turned away in disgust.

The next day the three knights and two squires rode away, leaving the Three Questing Ladies as they had found them, waiting for the next knights to take in search of adventures. They rode southwest toward Camelot. Sir Marhault rode toward Cornwall, but Camelot was on the way, and Gawain and Tor promised that King Arthur would welcome him to court. Gawain was still often quiet, but he wore his sorrow more easily now, so that it no longer drew attention to itself but rather seemed a part of his nature. Perhaps it was, Terence thought.

If Gawain had changed in the three months since they were all together, so had the others. Sir Marhault, like Gawain, was more thoughtful and more reluctant to make small talk. As for Tor, his face (which was thinner than before) and the way he held his shoulders (which were broader) both showed a greater self-assurance than Terence remembered. Even the caustic Plogrun had altered: he was more subdued and respectful to Tor. The dwarf was much more respectful to his fellow squire as well, and Terence wondered if perhaps he had changed himself.

One evening, as the October sun lowered over the open heath before them, they came upon a strange scene. A lady stood unsteadily between two figures who danced around her. On her one side was a tall knight in glittering armour, his open visor revealing a classically handsome face framed by shining golden curls. On the woman's other side was a dwarf with a wart on his cheek and straight black bristly hair that looked as if it belonged on a boar. The knight held a sword and glared at the dwarf, while the little man dodged nimbly around the woman, shrilly taunting him. Gawain, Tor and Sir Marhault looked at each other, then rode near to the squabbling group.

"You don't love her, you overgrown ninny!" the dwarf squealed. "You don't know what love is!"

"I tell you, I do love her," the knight snapped through clenched teeth. "I live but to do her service. And the first service I shall do her is to rid her of a pestilential little gnat."

The dwarf sneered and said, "Bah! That's all you want? To do her service? Is that the sort of namby-pamby foolishness that you call love? Ugh!" He made a long crude noise at the knight.

"Disgusting little beast!" the knight exclaimed.

Through all of this the lady in the middle simply wrung her hands and looked dismayed. She looked despairingly at the approaching riders, as if wondering who else was going to distress her. The dwarf glanced at the three knights and snorted, but after a moment he pursed his lips and nodded.

"Here now, Sir Bedbug, let's see if we can solve our brangle peaceable," the dwarf said. "Let these knights judge between us."

The knight's handsome lips tightened when the dwarf said his name, but he nodded and turned toward the approaching cavalcade. "Sir knights," he called in a ringing voice, "I ask your favour. Will you judge a dispute for us?"

Tor looked at Gawain, but Gawain said nothing. Sir Marhault said, "We shall do what we can, friend knight. Tell us your case."

"Wait just a moment, there," the dwarf interrupted. "Before we go any further, let's have a promise. Sir Bedbug, if they judge against you, will you pike off?"

The knight's nostrils flared, but he did not look at the dwarf. "I will accept their decision," he said.

"I'll pike off, too," the dwarf said promptly.

"Then I shall begin," the knight said. "I am Sir Edgar, whom men call The Fair. My lands lie all around this plain, and my castle, the noblest castle of these parts, lies on the River Sabrina. I offer this woman all my heart and life and service as long as we both shall live. This is my case."

"And I," said the dwarf, "am Bigglesnog the dwarf, of the town of Gloucester. I love the Lady Dulphina. That's my case."

"What manner of judgment do you want?" Sir Marhault inquired.

"Choose which one of us the lady shall have, stupid," Bigglesnog said.

Sir Marhault looked hard at the dwarf for a moment, then turned his horse toward Tor and Gawain. "Never have I been asked to perform so easy a task," he said.

"Well, it does seem fairly clear at this point," Tor agreed. "I've nothing against dwarfs, but I've never heard of one marrying a . . . one who isn't a dwarf." He looked inquiringly at his squire.

"And you won't either, sir," Plogrun snapped. "I know that you tall 'uns mostly think we dwarfs are ugly, but it works the other way as well. The thought of a true dwarf taking up with a woman like that fair turns my blood cold, it does. I don't hold with marrying outside one's own kind, and I never did! If you ask my advice, sir, I say give her to the knight."

"Well, that's what we'll have to do," Tor agreed. "She's beautiful; he's handsome. She's got style; he's got wealth. They could have been made for each other."

"It hardly seems a question to me," Sir Marhault mused. "Master . . . er . . . Bigglesnog, how comes it that you love this lady?"

"None of your business, pokenose."

Sir Marhault and Tor stared at the dwarf, then looked at each other.

"I should have added that the lady is genteel and the knight has manners," Tor commented.

"The dwarf is certainly doing his best to make this task easier," Sir Marhault agreed.

"He's an ill-mannered boor, sir," Plogrun said, looking with disfavour on Bigglesnog.

Gawain cleared his throat and said, "I assume that the point is to make the maiden happy?" Sir Marhault and Tor nodded. "Will you let me handle this, then?" The other two knights looked at him, a bit surprised, but after a second both nodded. Gawain rode a few steps closer and spoke to the lady. "Lady Dulphina? I bid you good day."

"Good . . . good day, sir knight." She faltered, looking at Gawain fearfully.

"It must be terribly uncomfortable for you to be in the midst of all this contention," Gawain said pleasantly. Some of the fear in her eyes eased and she nodded vigorously. "Will you let me help you, my lady?" he asked.

"Will you?" she asked in a small voice.

"I will," Gawain said with a smile. "First, my lady, I vow to you that you shall be forced to marry no one against your will. Now, my lady, do you love one of these suitors?"

"Oh yes, sir," she said.

"Then go to the one whom you love, and you shall have him."

Her eyes leaped joyfully, and she cried, "Oh, thank you, sir!" Without hesitation she turned to the dwarf and picked him up in her arms. They embraced ecstatically. Sir Edgar was aghast, and Sir Marhault, Tor and Plogrun patently astonished. Gawain grinned and winked at Terence.

"By all that's holy, Gawain!" Tor exclaimed. "How did you know?"

"I didn't, but I thought it my duty to protect the maiden's interests." A faint smile curled his lips as he turned back to the odd lovers and said, "Off with you now." Beaming happily, the lady and the dwarf mounted and rode away.

Sir Edgar sputtered angrily and raised his sword toward Gawain, but Gawain ignored him. He touched Guingalet with his heel and trotted ahead, leaving Tor and Sir Marhault with the seething knight. Terence urged his horse forward beside his master. The sorrow was still in Gawain's face, but a new gleam lit his eyes.

"Milord?"

"Yes, Terence?"

"Did it help?"

Gawain understood perfectly. "Ay, lad. So long as I carry the burden of The Maiden's Knight, she's not so far away as I thought."

They camped that night near a small clear pool beneath a little waterfall. After dinner, the knights sat around the fire talking. Plogrun leaned against a tree, smoked his pipe, and listened to the knights, but Terence felt oddly restless. After a few moments, he slipped into the woods. The moon was almost full, and in its gentle white glow even the darkest shadows seemed cheerful and comforting. Terence felt his restlessness ease out of him. With a satisfied smile, he sat on a rock next to the little pool and watched the stream tumble over itself then gurgle away.

"Peaceful, eh?" a voice asked pleasantly. Terence was vaguely aware of a shadow moving to his left, but he did not turn. He knew Robin's voice by now. "Nothing like the water for peacefulness," Robin continued. "Nothing so strong as the ocean, so friendly as a stream, so exciting as a fountain. Now that you've been to the Other World, you've seen that, haven't you?"

After a moment, Terence said, "We did cross through the water to get there. I will miss that world."

"Ay, you've already seen that you and your master aren't quite at home in this world, at least not like before." Terence nodded slowly. "It'll only get stronger, too," Robin continued. "Soon you'll find yourself looking into people's eyes to see if they've been there. And once you find someone who has, you'll greet him as a long-lost friend and take him to your heart."

Terence knew the faery was right. As much as he liked and admired people like Tor, he was closer to this unknown imp than he ever could be to Tor simply because Robin had been *there*. "But Robin," he said, "not everyone from the Other World is . . . friendly."

"Ay, my friend. There are the others. In fact, that's why I have come. I'm to tell you to be watchful." Then Terence knew that Robin was gone.

The bushes behind his perch rustled, and Gawain stepped out. "There you are," he said simply.

"Hello, milord," Terence said. Gawain stepped up next to Terence's rock and looked at the waterfall. Heavily and a bit clumsily, he put his hand on Terence's shoulder. "The others go to bed already, milord?" Terence asked.

Gawain shook his head. "There was no bearing it any longer, lad. Swords and horses and lances and tournaments. Once I would have talked until dawn, but now—" He did not finish. They watched the water together. The shadows shifted as the moon rose, but the water stayed the same.

"We'd better go back, milord, or they'll be wondering," Terence said at last.

"They're wondering already, lad."

"I know, but we needn't make it worse."

Gawain nodded. He tightened his grip on Terence's shoulder once, then let go and turned away. Terence slid off his rock and fell into step behind his master.

"Sir Gawain?" whispered a voice. Both turned around. Seated on a rock beneath the tumbling water was Nimue, her long black hair streaming around her. In the earth next to the rock, where Gawain had stood a moment before, a gleaming sword quivered. It was long and straight and cold-looking, and its black hilt was sombre and unjewelled. Nimue smiled affectionately and spoke in a voice that was difficult to distinguish from the sound of the falling water. "It is yours, my lord. It is the Sword Galatine."

"Why?" Gawain whispered.

"It is all that I have to give to my mistress's beloved," she said. The waterfall engulfed her in its spray, and she seemed to dissolve into the little pool. Gawain drew his old sword from its scabbard and threw it into the pond; then he pulled the Sword Galatine cleanly from the earth. He slipped it into his scabbard, and without looking back he and Terence returned to their camp.

12

THE ENCHANTRESS

Interesting news travels faster than knights on horseback, and when the three knights and two squires finally rode up the hill to Camelot, they found a crowd of courtiers and ladies and minstrels gathered to welcome them home. Across the courtyard, in a little pavilion, sat King Arthur and Queen Guinevere. The king stood and held out his hands in delight.

"Sir Tor! Sir Gawain! Welcome back to Camelot!" he called. "The reports of your deeds have not ceased since you left! You have brought honour to my court!"

Tor flushed deeply. All five of the travellers dismounted and knelt before King Arthur. Gawain said, "If that is so, then we are well pleased, my liege."

"Stand up! Stand up!" Arthur protested. "I want to hear the rest of your tales – and to meet this noble knight you have brought with you."

"This is Sir Marhault of Cornwall, sire," Gawain said, standing. "He is as skilful a knight as I have encountered and one of much compassion."

"He is welcome!" the king said. "We have received a stream of most unusual messengers from you," he added, laughing, "bearing dead animals, live animals, heads bound in magical cords, and I forget the rest. Tonight we shall feast in the great hall where your quests began, and you shall tell us your tales."

There were more greetings, more speeches, and more compliments, but at last Gawain and Terence were free to repair alone to Gawain's chambers and close the door behind them. The rooms were dusty and cold, but when Terence had lit a fire in the hearth, they were able to sprawl comfortably in two armchairs and relax.

"It isn't really home here any more," Gawain commented. "But at least here we can be away from the throng."

Terence nodded, and the two friends sat in comfortable silence, their thoughts in a different world, for about half an hour. Then came two sharp raps at the door, and Sir Kai stepped into the room.

"Gawain," Sir Kai said. He frowned slightly at Terence, and Terence remembered that at court squires did not sit in the presence of their masters. He stood quickly and moved to his squirely position behind Gawain's chair.

"Come in, Kai," Gawain said. "Sit with us . . . with me for a while."

Sir Kai nodded curtly and moved to the chair Terence had vacated. Again he glanced at Terence. "I didn't know your woodsman would be with you," he said at last.

Gawain smiled perfunctorily and said, "Didn't you?"

Sir Kai scowled. "Do you trust him?"

"With my life. More than once."

"Can you trust him to hold his tongue, though?"

Gawain looked up at Terence with laughter growing in his eyes. Terence grinned and looked down. "Yes," Gawain said simply.

Sir Kai had not missed the exchange of looks. "Oh, ay, I see," he said. "You already have some secrets between you. All right, then." He took a breath. "I'm glad to have you back, Gawain. Arthur needs you." Gawain was silent. "And he trusts you. He needs more people to trust."

"Are there so few?"

Kai frowned, and after a moment said, "Less than few. Oh, I don't mean to say he's surrounded by traitors. Only by fools."

"He has you and Merlin. Seems that should be—"

Sir Kai interrupted. "Merlin's gone."

Terence's head jerked up. "Merlin's gone already?" he exclaimed without thinking.

Gawain and Sir Kai both stared at Terence. "Did you know he would be leaving, lad?" Gawain asked.

"I . . . I must have heard him mention it one time, milord," Terence said lamely.

Gawain's eyes narrowed suspiciously, but Sir Kai grunted, "Ay, he may have. Arthur says he's known for some time that this was coming, but it's been a blow all the same."

"Where did Merlin go?"

"I don't know. He just announced one day that he'd done here, and he was off to take his rest. He walked out of the gates and met a lady – a faery beauty if I know anything – on a white horse. They rode away together."

"A lady on a white horse?"

"Never seen her like. Long black hair, white robes, green girdle. Half the fools of the court rode off after them to find out her name."

"Did they?"

"No. They followed her north to the lake lands and then the trail disappeared."

"Ay, it would," Gawain said.

"You know her?"

"I think she's the Lady of the Lake," Gawain said, his eyes again meeting Terence's. Terence nodded. So Nimue had come to take Merlin home. It was as Ganscotter had said: the faeries never forget their own.

"Hmm. It's what Arthur thought, too," Sir Kai said. "Arthur says he's glad for Merlin, but he misses him like the devil. He's lonely now."

"Lonely? But he's just married," Gawain said gently.

Sir Kai's lips curled. "Ay, Guinevere. She'll be no help to Arthur. She looks pretty enough in a wedding dress, and I'll grant she cares for Arthur, but she seems almost afraid to come near him. She can't help him like that."

"It must be hard to be wife to a king," Gawain commented.

"Not as hard as to be a king without friend or counsellor," Sir Kai snapped.

"He has you," Gawain said.

"I'm no Merlin. Arthur's feeling the weight of

ruling more. And it's changing him. He tires easily these days."

"Arthur tired?" Gawain asked, surprised. "I've never seen that before. He seemed himself when he greeted us."

"Ay," Sir Kai grunted. He stood to take his leave. "It did him that much good to see you again." He stopped by the door, as if he had something else to say, but at last he only scowled. "As I say, I'm glad you're back," he muttered, and left.

At the banquet that night, Terence stood behind Gawain's chair at the head table, beside the king, and listened to Gawain recount their adventures. This was now the third time that he had heard Gawain tell the tale, but each time the story was different. Where Gawain had told the complete but simple and unadorned story to Ganscotter and a brief and very selective summary to Tor and Sir Marhault, this time he told the tale in flowing courtly language, filled with colourful descriptions of armour and costumes and often describing knights as "doughty warriors" or "passing good knights" or "villainous recreants". It all sounded very strange coming from Gawain, but he certainly made even very brief and humdrum events sound noble and inspiring. When Gawain told how he had killed Ablamor's wife, several ladies, including Queen Guinevere, looked appalled. Gawain himself was grim, and Arthur closed his eyes for a few moments, as if he shared Gawain's pain.

Gawain did not tell everything, of course. As Terence expected, he left Nimue out of the story of Pelleas and Ettard, and though he told of being in a faery castle owned by a great enchanter, he did not give Ganscotter's name nor mention that the enchanter had a daughter. Burdens given in the Other World were not to be recounted merely for an evening's courtly entertainment.

The king closed his eyes again, this time for longer, and Terence began to watch Arthur more closely. When the banquet had begun, the king had seemed as strong as ever, but as the evening wore on, he had grown more silent. When Gawain finished his tale, the king raised his hand and said, "Sir Gawain, you tell a tale of glory but also of regret. I honour your telling of it. Now," he said, "Sir Marhault will tell us of his adventures." Arthur gestured mildly toward Sir Marhault, and his hand knocked over a goblet, splashing the table and the queen's gown with wine. The king stood unsteadily, apologizing to Guinevere, and Terence suddenly saw how the king would look when he was old. Now he knew that something was wrong.

Guinevere smiled reassuringly to Arthur, but there was concern in her eyes. Bridging the awkward pause in the festivities, Sir Marhault began his tale, but Terence was thinking furiously and did not hear. Ganscotter's description of The Enchantress had returned to him – "First she must remove the world's kings and princes" – and he remembered the woman in the fog saying that she would act after Merlin was gone. Terence began to fidget, wishing to be away, though he knew not where. Then, quietly and simply, the king lowered his chin and fainted onto the table in front of him.

Knights and servants rushed to help him, and Terence backed away toward the door. He waited only long enough to hear someone say that Arthur was alive before he turned and ran. He leaped down the stairs to the great courtyard and ran to the stables. There, in a large corner stall, stood Guingalet, eyeing Terence suspiciously. Terence did not hesitate. Climbing over the stall, he threw a blanket on Guingalet's back and straightened it. The black horse reared and kicked, but Terence avoided the hooves and threw Gawain's saddle on Guingalet's back. Tightening the saddle took time, as Terence had to dodge the horse's teeth and heels, but at last it was in place. Terence was just grabbing a bridle, when Gawain's voice called out,

"Terence!"

Gawain stood in the open door of the stable. He still wore his feasting clothes, but he carried the Sword Galatine. "I have to go, milord," Terence gasped, trying to fit the bridle over Guingalet's tossing head. "And it may be far. My own horse may not make it."

Gawain stepped forward and took the bridle roughly from Terence's hand. "Where, lad?"

Terence shook his head. "I'll know it when I see it."

"Is it for the king?" Gawain demanded. Terence nodded, and Gawain quickly caught the horse's head and slipped the bridle over it. "I'll go with you. Guingalet will carry us both."

"I don't think you should," Terence said. "I . . . may find something you won't like." Terence could not bring himself to tell Gawain about The Enchantress, particularly about his own suspicions concerning her.

"I'm sure I won't," Gawain said. "But you're not leaving without me all the same. What will you do if Guingalet throws you?"

"Milord, please—"

"No, Terence. I know that this is your task, beyond my strength. But let me go as your escort. When we arrive, I'll do what you say. I promise."

213

With no time to argue, and secretly glad of Gawain's company, Terence agreed, and they climbed onto Guingalet. Terence sat in front of Gawain, almost on the horse's black neck, and Gawain held the reins. "Out of the gates, milord," Terence said. "And then north, I think." Gawain began Guingalet at a fast trot, but Terence shook his head. "No, milord. Spring him."

"We'll wear him out," Gawain warned.

"I know, but we can't get where we're going by pacing ourselves. Top speed, milord."

Gawain booted the horse into a dead run. Terence wound his fingers into Guingalet's thick mane and held on. Ahead loomed the black mass of the forest, and then they were into the shadows. Slim, leafless branches whipped and cut Terence's face, and Gawain shouted, "This is mad, Terence!" but still he urged Guingalet on. A repugnant feeling, like a smell of decay, began to grow in Terence's breast, and he aimed himself toward the source of the feeling. "Left, milord. To the left a hair. More. There! Now straight ahead, and faster!"

The shadows leaped and danced around them as they careered over meadows and crashed through brush. Terence's heart pounded in time to the drumming of Guingalet's hooves. The sky was clouded and heavy, but here and there the clouds broke and let through a cold moonlight that silvered the trees and etched sharper shadows on their trunks. One moonlit copse, dappled with black shadows, looked to Terence like the face of his messenger friend Robin, but there was no mischief or merriment in the face's expression. A few hoofbeats and a heartbeat, and it was past.

Time passed like time in a dream, sometimes an hour flitting by in a second, sometimes a single step lasting an age. "How much longer, Terence?" cried Gawain.

"I don't know," Terence called back. "Into those hills . . . no! That hill! With the treeless top!" Before them rose a small chain of rounded hills, mostly wooded, and at their very centre was one hill taller than the rest, bald of tree cover. "The feeling is coming from there, I think."

Gawain did not ask what Terence meant by "the feeling". He only adjusted their course and urged Guingalet on for a final race up the hill, crooning to the aughisky in a language that Terence did not understand. Guingalet's breath was laboured, but he did not slow, and soon Terence could see the summit of the hill and, at the very top, a winking of firelight.

A minute – or an hour – passed, and they burst

out of the trees into the open area at the top of the hill. Terence leaped from Guingalet's back to stand between Gawain and the scene that met their eyes. Before him was a round pool, lined with hewn stones and filled with still water. At the edge of the cistern, a black cauldron bubbled over a fire, and beside the cauldron knelt the woman that Terence had seen in the pond and in the night fog. Behind the woman, still silent, stood the knight who always accompanied her. The woman leaped to her feet as Terence and Gawain arrived and stared first at Gawain, still on horseback.

"Gawain," she breathed.

Then Terence's fears were realized, and he heard Gawain whisper, "Mother." Then the silent knight stepped forward into the firelight, and Gawain choked. "Father?" he gasped. "But I buried you myself."

The knight did not answer, and Gawain's mother turned her attention to Terence. A light of recognition flamed in her eyes, and she hissed, "You! Who are you? I thought I knew all the great sorcerers, but who are you?"

Terence did not speak, and at last Gawain answered, "This is my squire, Mother."

Morgause ignored her son. "I must know," she said. "Who are you?" Her voice was almost a scream.

"I am a servant," Terence answered. "That is all. I serve your son, and I serve King Arthur."

The blaze of hatred in her eyes seemed to outshine the fire. Morgause spoke over her shoulder to the silent knight. "Kill him."

The knight drew his long sword and walked around the pool toward Terence. Terence heard Gawain dismount behind him, but he did not look back, nor did he move. "Milord?" Terence said quietly.

"It's my father, lad. I know that armour as I know my own."

"I need your help," Terence said.

The silent knight stopped before Terence and raised his sword over his head. Terence turned away from the knight and looked into the spiteful eyes of Morgause. He could feel no fear of a mere sword before the more horrible, more terrifying figure of this woman. He sensed rather than saw the knight begin his swing, and then the night calm was broken by a terrific clash as Gawain stepped between them and parried the blow with the Sword Galatine. Terence stepped toward Morgause, hardly able to breathe, as the sound of steel on steel continued behind him.

"What is your name?" Morgause whispered fiercely, almost desperately. "You are no ordinary magician."

"I am a squire," Terence said. It was hard to speak.

"Do you take me for a fool?" she shrieked. "I concealed myself from my own sister Morgan, from Merlin, from the whole cursed Seelie Court. Only you saw my preparations. Only you heard my plans. Are you Merlin's disciple?" Terence shook his head and stepped closer. Her fury grew. "Do you know who I am?"

"You are Gawain's mother. Morgause," Terence said.

"Is that all you know?" she laughed. "Have you never heard of The Enchantress?"

Terence nodded. "Ganscotter told me," he managed to say.

At the name, Morgause's eyes widened, and for a moment her fury was clouded by fear. Behind him, Terence heard Gawain grunt as he parried blow after blow. "Then he told you who I am?" she demanded.

The words came to Terence, and the knot in his throat loosened. "No. How could he? How could you be The Enchantress? Look at your little pot bubbling. You are only a petty witch."

Morgause screamed with indescribable fury, and flecks of foam appeared on her lips. "Would you like to see my little pot, then?" she shrieked. She threw a handful of dust into the cauldron, and then the air filled with thick, yellowish-green smoke. Terence coughed and felt nauseated, and he heard Gawain choking in the cloud behind him. Eyes watering, Terence backed away, seeking a place where he could see. Morgause laughed shrilly, but Terence could no longer see her. The sound of sword on sword ceased, and there were only sporadic thuds from the battleground.

"Milord!" Terence shouted, filled with horror. There was no answer.

At last the smoke thinned and in the haze Terence saw the silent knight, huge against the night sky, holding Gawain high above his head with one hand. Both knights still held their swords, but Gawain's hung limply. Gawain's face was ashen with weariness and pain and from the gangrenous smell of the smoke. The knight stepped to the edge of the pool and held Gawain over the black water. From across the pool came Morgause's harsh voice, "Throw him in to die."

Gawain raised the Sword Galatine high once more to give one final, futile blow before he died, and at that moment the sun appeared over the edge of the eastern forest. A shaft of sunlight touched the tip of the Sword Galatine and showered a rainbow of reflected light around the clearing. Before Terence's awed eyes, Gawain's strength grew. A new light flashed in his eyes, and he seemed almost to grow bigger. He tightened his grip on his sword and struck the silent knight with all the force that had just filled him. The Sword Galatine clove through the solid plate armour, from the left shoulder to the right side, and the armour collapsed in a heap, with Gawain on top of the pile. The armour was empty.

Morgause, across the pool, stood immobile, and in that moment Terence leaped forward to the still bubbling cauldron and pushed it over. His right hand blistered on the hot iron, but he kept pushing until the pot had emptied all its contents into the still pool. Morgause shrieked as if dying and leaped forward to save the pot, but she was too late and tumbled into the pool herself and disappeared below the surface.

For a moment, the pool was still. Then the waters began to roil and swirl. The surface rounded and swelled, as if boiling, and then from the very centre of the pool burst a fountain of frothy white water. Spray from the fountain freshened the air, drove away the last of the sickly yellow smoke, and reached up into the bright ray of the new sun. The pool filled to the top with water and began to flow over the hewn stones that lined the edge. One by one, the stones loosened and fell into the expanding pool, and the spreading waters found a channel and began flowing down the hill. Of Morgause there was no sign.

"Milord?" Terence called, stumbling over to his master's side. Gawain was breathing but unconscious. Terence pulled his master's body away from the expanding edges of the fountain pool, then watched the waters cover the crushed empty armour that Gawain had fought.

"It wasn't really his father, you know," came a familiar voice.

"Hello Robin," Terence said, his face lightening. "You know, I thought it might not be. But I do thank you for telling me."

"Oh, ay, you're such an expert now. You probably don't need me at all. I'll just take myself off, then." Robin sniffed in wounded dignity.

"As if I could get rid of you that easily." Terence grinned. "Was that you during the night?"

"Beside you all the way. You ride hard, young master." Robin gestured at Terence's hand. "You'll want some salve on that."

For the next few minutes Robin anointed and

bound Terence's scarred and swollen palm. When it was bandaged, Terence asked, "And what of Morgause? Is she dead?"

"I don't know. But her spell is broken. Arthur's getting better as we speak." Robin suddenly began to chuckle. "'Petty witch' indeed! That properly floored her, it did. You've got your share of gall, young master."

"That's twice you've called me 'young master'. What do you mean?"

Robin smiled. "You told me once that if I ever found out who you were, I should tell you. Now I know." Terence felt still inside, and a wide gulf of waiting passed between the two friends. "Your father told me," Robin added.

"Who is my father?" Terence whispered.

"Have you not guessed?" Terence shook his head, and Robin said, "Ganscotter himself." And then Robin knelt at Terence's feet. "Young master, I am bidden to invite you back to your father's court. You have done well. He says that now at last you may dwell in your own world."

Terence felt a pure joy welling up within, but he gestured toward his unconscious master. "And Gawain?" Robin shook his head, and Terence replied immediately. "Then I shall stay here."

Robin stood, grinning. "He said you would. He

also said I might visit you now and again, if it's convenient for you, of course."

"Huh, much you care for that," Terence retorted, but he nodded.

"And now," Robin said, "you need a way back to Camelot. May I? I'll have you back home – and your horse, too – in a trice." With a wink and a wave, Robin disappeared. In a moment, the bright fountain at the top of the hill grew small and distant, and Terence found himself and Gawain back in Gawain's chambers at Camelot. He was damp and weary beyond words, but he bundled the still unconscious Gawain into bed and even went down to the stables to rub down the exhausted and confused Guingalet before he slept himself.

Gawain slept most of that day, but Terence's burned hand woke him after only a few hours. He rose and changed Robin's dressing. Then he visited the kitchens and listened to the scullery maids chatter about the king's miraculous recovery. When Gawain stirred at last, Terence had a fire on the hearth and a simple meal laid out waiting. Gawain looked about his bed, bemused.

"I've either had a very strange dream," he said, "or you've some explaining to do, lad."

Terence's eyes twinkled. "Have you been

dreaming of the bogey man, then? Shall I protect you?"

"Faith, lad, I think you could. What happened?" Gawain sat up abruptly and said, "Arthur!"

"He's fine, milord," Terence reassured him. "The spell is broken."

Gawain relaxed and then, after a moment, said, "Was it my mother all along?"

"Yes."

"How long have you known about this spell of hers?"

"Since sometime on our journey. But I wasn't sure it was your mother until last night."

"And the knight I fought?"

"Another spell. Nothing but your father's empty armour."

Gawain closed his eyes and sighed, then asked, "Where is my mother?"

"I don't know, milord. Her spell was broken when I pushed her cauldron over into the water. She fell in too and then just disappeared." Terence told Gawain how the still black pool had become a gushing fresh fountain and stream. "But the important thing is that her enchantment was destroyed," Terence concluded.

Gawain nodded toward Terence's bandage. "From the cauldron?"

Terence shrugged. "I hardly feel it now."

"Of course," Gawain agreed solemnly. "And how did we come home? No, never mind. You know, but you probably can't explain it to me. After all, I only have a trace of faery blood. And you have . . . Have you ever found out how much faery blood you have?"

"Half, milord. On my father's side." Terence turned to the meal he had prepared. "Shall we eat?"

Gawain nodded, but before joining Terence by the fire he opened a cabinet and withdrew a bottle of wine and two pewter goblets. "And drink together, I think."

Terence thought of Sir Kai's surprise at seeing Terence seated in his master's presence and said, "What if some courtier comes by and sees you drinking with me?"

Gawain grinned. "What if some faery comes by and sees you drinking with me? Who would be more shocked?" He poured the wine, and they ate together by the fire.

They were still sitting together an hour later when a soft knock came from the door and King Arthur entered.

They both leaped to their feet, and Gawain said, "My liege! I am glad to see you so restored."

In truth, Arthur looked like a different man than the tired king who had fainted at the banquet only the previous evening. The king smiled politely and said, "Thank you. I feel better than I have for weeks. Please, sit down, Nephew." Gawain lowered himself back into his chair, and Terence took his position behind his master, still holding his goblet of wine. Arthur looked at the goblet, and his eyes twinkled.

"I have come, Gawain, because I had a most curious dream last night while the doctors held my hand and argued about how soon I should die. I was delirious, no doubt, but I remember that you were in this dream. And you, too, Squire Terence."

"Indeed, sire?" Gawain asked politely.

"Yes," Arthur nodded. "There was also a silent knight and a . . . an enchantress of some sort."

"I have had dreams of that sort, my liege," Gawain said, nodding slowly. "Perhaps it was the brandy."

"I shall speak to the wine steward," Arthur said gravely. "I do not know how the dream ended, for I awoke suddenly, feeling much refreshed. I suppose that you were present in my dreams because I am so very delighted to have you back in my court. Thank you both for your service."

Gawain knelt and said, "Our service is always

yours, sire."

"Even in my dreams?" Arthur asked.

"Especially there, O king," Terence murmured, bowing.

As he raised his head again, Terence caught his breath. He suddenly realized that without thinking he had bowed to King Arthur slightly and from the waist only, as a great lord might bow to an equal, not deeply and bending the knees, as a servant bows to his master. He prepared to stammer an apology, but before he could speak the king returned his bow, with exactly the same inflection. Gawain raised his eyebrows, but Arthur only smiled again and took his leave.

"I'll stir up the fire and fetch some more wine, milord," Terence said hurriedly.

AUTHOR'S NOTE

Some of the best stories are the old ones, the tales that have been told by generations of storytellers. In English, the stories about King Arthur and the knights who gathered at his Round Table are among the best loved. They have been told and retold continuously for a thousand years. Among these are many that tell about Arthur's nephew, Sir Gawain. While much of this book is my own invention – the character of my hero, Terence, for instance – many of the events and characters are from a few of those old tales about Sir Gawain.

Some of these stories I borrowed from *Le Morte d'Arthur*, a great volume of Arthurian legends collected in 1485 by Sir Thomas Malory. Books III and IV of Malory's collection tell about Sir Tor, about the hart and hound at the wedding feast, about the rebellion of the five kings, about the three questing ladies, and about Gawain's involvement in the love affair between Pelleas and Ettard. The story of Gawain's choice, when he was permitted to choose whether his lady should be beautiful or hideous, is another of the old tales, though it does not appear in Malory's collection.

Of course, stories that have been recounted so often by so many tellers will take many different forms. Even familiar characters in the stories change from telling to telling. In most of the early legends, Gawain is the greatest of all of Arthur's knights. One beautiful poetic story, *Sir Gawain and the Green Knight*, says of Sir Gawain, "Of all knights on earth most honoured is he." By the time of Sir Thomas Malory's book, though, the greatest of all Arthur's knights was Sir Lancelot, and to hear Malory tell it, Gawain was a rather coarse and selfish knight of only moderate skill. (At one point, Malory even provides a helpful list of all the knights who defeated Sir Gawain in battle.)

Now I have nothing against Sir Lancelot – well, not much – but I've never approved of Gawain's demotion. The courteous and humble knight whom I encountered and loved in such poems as *Sir Gawain and the Green Knight* bears little resemblance to Malory's sullen Gawain. Of course, as a storyteller, Malory is free to say what he likes about his characters, but other storytellers have the same freedom. And so, I have retold the same stories that Malory tells, but I have told them in a different way, trying to restore the reputation of this most honoured of all knights on earth.

G.M

THE SQUIRE, HIS KNIGHT AND HIS LADY

GERALD MORRIS

Squire Terence and Sir Gawain are off questing again,
but this time they have a grim destination. Gawain is set
to meet the Green Knight in a contest that will surely
end in his death. Along the way, the knight and his squire
have a slew of hair-raising adventures and meet a feisty
damsel-in-distress named Eileen. As they weave their way
between the world of men and the faery world, Terence
finds love and Gawain confronts the true nature of
honour and courage.

ISBN 0 7534 1032 X

THE SAVAGE DAMSEL
AND THE DWARF

GERALD MORRIS

Her family's castle besieged by an evil knight, Lady Lynet
sets out for King Arthur's court, accompanied by a strange
dwarf, Roger, to recruit a rescuer. But the only person who
volunteers to help is a scruffy serving boy, Beaumains. The
three travel to Lynet's castle, encountering danger, magic
and many unusual characters, including the famous knight
Gawain and his squire, Terence. Through their amazing
adventures, Lynet discovers that people can be far more
than they seem, and surprises even herself.

ISBN 0 7534 1048 6

THE SQUIRE'S TALES

BOOK IV

PARSIFAL'S PAGE

GERALD MORRIS

Piers is desperate to become a knight's page and escape the dirt and noise of his father's blacksmith shop. But Parsifal, the aspiring knight that he serves, is not the sort of master he had in mind. Although brave and strong, Parsifal is unschooled in courtly behaviour. On their adventure-filled travels, Piers slowly begins to realize that being a knight has nothing to do with shining armour and tournament victories. As they quest for the elusive Holy Grail, Piers and Parsifal learn about the true nature of knighthood – and about themselves.

ISBN 0 7534 1008 7